SOMETHING SUSPICIOUS

SOMETHING SUSPICIOUS

Kathryn Osebold Galbraith

AN AVON CAMELOT BOOK

AVON BOOKS
A division of
The Hearst Corporation
1790 Broadway
New York, New York 10019

The Atheneum edition contains the following Library of Congress Cataloging
in Publication Data:

Galbraith, Kathryn Osebold.
    Something suspicious.

    "A Margaret K. McElderry book."
    Summary: Lizzie and her best friend try to track down a bank robber called
the Green Pillowcase Bandit and end up with more mysteries than they can
handle.
    1. Children's stories, American.   [1. Robbers and outlaws—Fiction.
2. Mystery and detective stories]   I. Title.
PZ7.G13035o   1985   [Fic]   85-4003

First Camelot Printing: January 1987

To Elissa, Amy, & Jenny,
Jeff, Lisa, & Mindy,
Jennifer & Lindsay.
And once again to Steve.

Contents

One

Something Happens

Come on, Ivy, answer. I held the phone away from my ear and let it ring about fifty million times. Come on, *please*.

"Lizzie, are you on the phone again?"

"No." I hung up and wandered into the dining room. Mom was sitting at the long table in front of a pile of books.

"Ivy's not home yet." I flopped down in the chair next to her. "I even called the operator and made sure I had the right number." Ivy Frances Featherstone is my very best friend and I couldn't wait to see her. It had been a whole year—well, a whole school year—since her last visit.

"Honey, this is just her first day home. You can call her tomorrow."

"Tomorrow! By tomorrow she could be flying to Paris, France, or Berlin, Germany, or Bangkok—" I forgot what country Bangkok was in. "Or London, England," I finished.

Mom didn't lift her head. "Lizzie, I'm sure she'll still be right here in Broadhead tomorrow morning. I just think Ivy and her dad might need a little time to get reacquainted."

Reacquainted. That sounded funny. I couldn't imagine

having to get reacquainted with Dad, but I guess for Ivy it's different. Ivy's parents are divorced and Ivy lives with both of them—just not at the same time. She lives in Chicago with her mother during the school year and spends her summers with her dad. Last June her father moved here, so now this is her summer home—if she ever gets here.

"I wasn't going to talk long," I said. "I was just going to ask her if she could sleep over tomorrow night."

No answer. I don't think Mom even heard me. A fly buzzed somewhere in the kitchen. I fiddled with the pens and pencils on the table until Mom reached over and covered them with her hand. Then I tried reading her book upside down. C-e-n-t-u-r-y. Something Century.

"Is that for school?" Mom used to sell real estate, but now she's gone back to college for her degree. I leaned over her shoulder to look at the book right side up. *"English Writers of the Nineteenth Century."* I made a face. "Is it good?"

"Yes." She wiggled her shoulder for me to move. "Come on, Lizzie. You can't be that bored. And you'll see Ivy tomorrow."

"I know, but there's nothing to do today." I waited, hoping she'd think of something. When she didn't answer, I tried again. "Did you know that people can die, actually die of boredom? It said so right in *Time* magazine." It didn't, but I'm sure it's true.

Mom reached for a pencil and started scribbling some notes on the back of an envelope. "I don't think you're about to die. Where's Mitch? Why don't you two go play tennis or something?"

"Oh, Mitch. He's worse than useless." I thumped the chair leg with my foot. "I should have had a sister instead of a brother. Ever since that Peabrain moved into this town, Mitch never has time to do anything with me anymore."

"Billy Hunt isn't so bad," Mom said. "You know, maybe if you stopped calling him Peabrain, you two might hit it off a little better."

I snorted. Who wanted to hit it off with a peabrain who called you Lizard?

"Well..." Mom finished her note and looked up. "Why don't you go uptown and get a haircut?"

"Uh-uh, not me." I shook my head. I was never going to get my hair cut again. I'm going to let it grow and grow until it's halfway down my back like Ivy's.

"Just a trim," Mom coaxed. "It would look so nice for tonight."

"Tonight?" I sat up. "Is something happening tonight?"

"Wendell Bennett is coming for dinner."

"Oh." I immediately lost interest. Mr. Bennett is just a friend of my parents. I gave the chair another thump. "You know what's wrong with this town? Nothing ever happens here. Ever!"

"Lizzie, I have forty more pages to read before dinner, so if you can't find anything to do..."

She didn't have to say anything more. "Okay, okay, I'm going."

I had to squeeze out the back screen door and step over Basil to get outside. Mom has made beds for Basil all over the porch, but he always goes back to his old spot right in front of the door.

Basil is a golden retriever. Dad says he's a fat golden retriever and that we should put him on a diet, but Basil's just a little greedy, that's all. Anyway, he's good company. *He* always listens to me.

"Here, Basil." I plunked down on the top step of the porch and patted my leg. Basil ambled over and sprawled out beside me. "I hope I never grow up," I told him. "Because when you're grown up, you don't even care if there's nothing to do." Basil's tail gave an answering wag. I sighed. I was so bored that even walking uptown and checking out the WANTED posters in the post office seemed like too much work.

Then I heard a voice that made me duck my head below the porch bushes. It was Delight Nelson, our next-door neighbor. Mrs. Nelson is really sort of nice, but once she starts talking, she never stops. Mitch says it's because she worked for the phone company for years and years before

3

she retired. We finally had to set up a phone system of our own. Now if one of us gets caught by her, someone else has to yell that they're wanted on the telephone.

"I wonder who she's got now?" I peeked around the bushes. Ha! It was Mitch. Served him right. She had caught him by the back fence, and now I could hear her bragging about her new cat, Missy Megs, and what a wonderful mouser Megs was. "She's the best hunter I've ever seen," Mrs. Nelson was saying. "She's always bringing me a little field mouse or a pesky mole."

"That's disgusting," I whispered to Basil. "I'm glad you don't do things like that."

When there was a split-second pause, Mitch said, "Are they still alive? The field mice, I mean?"

How gross. I couldn't believe this conversation, but Mrs. Nelson didn't seem to mind.

"Oh, sometimes," she said. "Megs doesn't mean to be cruel. It's just in a cat's nature to hunt."

When Mitch finally got away, I thought for sure he'd yell at me for leaving him stranded, but he didn't seem mad at all. In fact he seemed to be in a good mood. He came bounding up the porch steps and stopped to give Basil a tummy rub. Basil loved it; he wiggled around like a puppy.

Everyone says that Mitch and I look alike but we don't. I mean, we both have blond hair like Mom, but Mitch is miles taller than I am. And he's skinny. I'm not fat. I'm just big for my age.

"Hey, did you know that Mr. Bennett is coming for dinner? Maybe he'll give us some money." That was an old joke because Mr. Bennett is president of the National Bank of Broadhead.

Mitch shrugged. "I'm not going to be here anyway. I'm going over to Billy's for dinner." He gave Basil one final pat and disappeared into the house.

I glared after him. I don't know why I even bothered being nice to him anymore. "You just wait, Mitchell John Bruce," I yelled. "Ivy and I are going to have a terrific, exciting summer, and I'm not going to tell you a thing about it!"

That night I was the one elected to coax Basil into the basement before Mr. Bennett arrived. When Basil was a puppy, Mr. Bennett used to hide dog biscuits in his pockets for Basil to sniff out. When Basil grew up, Mr. Bennett forgot about the game, but Basil didn't. He still yelps and jumps all over Mr. Bennett whenever he sees him, so now we have to lock Basil away every time his old friend comes for a visit.

"Poor Basil." I could hear him whining at the basement door. I felt like a traitor.

"Poor Wendell," Mom said. We both giggled.

Mr. Bennett arrived at exactly seven-fifteen. I never knew Mrs. Bennett because she died a long time ago, but Mr. Bennett used to come over all the time until he took up cigars. Now Mom only invites him in the summer when she can have all the doors and windows open.

Dinner wasn't so bad. Mr. Bennett didn't pull out one of those brown cigars until dessert.

"Well, Stewart," he said to my father. He leaned back in his chair. "I don't mind telling you that I'm a little worried. I suppose you've heard about the bank robbery over at Green Hills."

Bank robbery? My head snapped up. I hadn't heard about any bank robbery.

"Bold as brass, he was," Mr. Bennett said. "He slipped into the bank wearing a ski mask and handed the teller a pillowcase. Told her to fill it up and got fifteen hundred dollars just like that." Mr. Bennett snapped his fingers. "The police have even given him a name—the Green Pillowcase Bandit. Guess they think that's his trademark or something."

The Green Pillowcase Bandit! "Do you think that could happen here?" I asked hopefully. "I mean, right here in Broadhead?"

Mr. Bennett looked surprised. I think he'd forgotten that I was still at the table.

"Well, we hope not, Lizzie." Then he laughed, and a big cloud of gray smoke came out of his mouth. "But I'm depending on you to keep a sharp eye out for him."

Dad laughed too, but I didn't think it was funny. Suppose I did see something suspicious? Suppose I just happened to be in the bank when—

"Lizzie." Mom was shaking her head at me as if she could tell what I was thinking. "You know Mr. Bennett is just teasing. I don't want you to even think about bank robbers or holdups or anything of the kind. You're so dramatic; the first thing you know, you'll be seeing robbers all over town."

That wasn't fair. Just because I have a healthy imagination—that's what Mr. Lancaster, my fourth grade teacher, told Mom—just because I have a healthy imagination, nobody believes a thing I say.

"And please don't tell Mitch," Mom added. "I'm sure Mr. Bennett told us this in confidence."

She nodded encouragingly. I nodded back. That part was easy. "I won't say a word to Mitch," I promised. But I didn't promise anything about Ivy. In fact, I couldn't wait to see her face when I told her that there was a bank robber loose and that he was headed—maybe—right for the Broadhead Bank!

Two

Making Plans

"Girls?"

There was a sudden knock on my bedroom door.

Oh-oh, that was Mom's voice. I didn't have to tell Ivy. She had already disappeared under the covers. I lifted the edge of the sheet and rolled the flashlight in after her.

"Girls, if I hear one more giggle in there tonight, I'm going to have to separate you two."

I peeked at Ivy. She was a big white lump under the sheets. I pinched my mouth together to keep from laughing.

Mom gave one more rap to show she meant business. "Now, good night. I'll see you in the morning."

I waited and counted to ten. Then just to be safe, I counted to ten again before I tapped Ivy on the back.

Ivy poked her head out. "Do you think she's really mad?" She sounded worried. That was the second time Mom had been up since we had gone to bed.

"Nope, not Mom." I pulled the flashlight back out and bounced its beam around the wall. "If she were really mad, she would have come busting right in."

When I called Ivy this morning, I'd been worried that maybe we'd have to get reacquainted too, but after about two seconds it felt as if she'd never been away. I waved the flashlight in front of her. "You know what we can use this for?" I was all ready to tell her about the Green Pillowcase Bandit, but Ivy shook her head.

"No, wait. Finish telling me about everybody else first."

That was just like Ivy. My mother said Ivy was very methodical. Ivy said she wasn't methodical. It was just that it made her dizzy the way I jumped from one thing to another.

"Okay." I stopped to swallow. I felt as if I'd been talking all night, trying to catch her up on everything that had happened since last summer.

"Who do you want to hear about next?" I'd already told her about Delight Nelson's new cat. Dad said the cat was a special breed called a Persian, but to me it looked like one of those huge white snowy owls in Mitch's bird book. It had the same hungry yellow eyes.

"What about Baby Imogene?"

Baby Imogene and her family lived two houses down, just on the other side of Mrs. Nelson.

"Well, she's got more hair now," I said, "but she still drools. Mrs. Morely said that maybe this summer she'll let us babysit for her. For money, I mean." I flopped back in the bed, shooting the beam straight up to the ceiling. "Gee, I'm glad you're back. I really missed you. And just wait until I tell you—"

Footsteps. I sat up. Was that Mom coming up the stairs again? I knew Ivy must be thinking the same thing because I couldn't hear her breathing.

A door opened across the hall and then snapped shut. A second later, I heard a muffled sound of music.

"It's okay," I whispered. "It's just Mitch." He didn't count.

"Mitch," Ivy repeated softly.

I twisted around. "Ivy Frances Featherstone, you promised! You promised that you didn't like him anymore, remember?"

"I know." But her voice was still soft.

I gave my pillow a thump. "It would just wreck the whole summer if you go back on your word. Remember the soap?"

I shook my head in disgust. Last summer Ivy had such a crush on Mitch that she swiped the bar of soap Mitch used to wash his hands. And then to make it even worse, she wadded it up in toilet paper and carried it with her everywhere. It seemed as if Ivy had smelled of Ivory soap for the entire summer.

"You don't have to worry about the soap," she said. She sat up and hugged her knees. "It dissolved. My mom forgot and threw my jeans in the wash. Even the toilet paper is gone."

"Good." That made me feel better. "He's too old for you anyway." Mitch is almost fourteen and Ivy's only eleven. I'm eleven too, but I'm an old eleven. "Besides, we're not going to have anything to do with Mitch this summer. He doesn't deserve it. If he wants to waste his time with Billy Peabrain Hunt, then let him!"

I'd already told Ivy all about Peabrain, right down to his dirty fingernails. "Anyway, we have more important things to talk about than Mitch and his dumb friend. Wait until you hear what I found out. But you have to promise not to tell. Promise?"

The room was too dark for me to see Ivy cross her heart, but I felt the bed jiggle.

"Promise."

"There's a bank robber loose," I whispered. "The Green Pillowcase Bandit! And he's headed right this way."

"A bank robber! Really?" she squeaked.

"Really. Mr. Bennett said so and he should know. He's the president of the bank." And then I told her word for word everything Mr. Bennett had said.

"But Lizzie, he didn't exactly say that the robber was coming here."

"Well, no. But he said he was really worried about it."

"Oh."

I didn't like the sound of that *oh*. "And he could be coming here. After all, he robbed the Green Hills bank and that isn't very far away."

"How far away is it?"

I didn't know, but I knew Ivy didn't know either. "Ten miles," I said.

When Ivy didn't answer, I said, "And Mr. Bennett did say he was depending on me to keep a sharp eye out for him."

The bedsprings jiggled again as Ivy settled down on her side of the bed. "We don't have to go *into* the bank, do we?"

What a funny question. "Sure, where else would you find a bank robber except in a bank?" I scrunched up my pillow under my head, but I was too excited to even think about going to sleep. "Just think if we were the ones to catch him. We'd be famous!"

"But maybe this bank robber has never even heard of Broadhead," Ivy said. "Maybe he's on his way to Detroit by now."

"I know, but still . . ." I sighed. "It sure would be exciting. We'd get our pictures on the front page of the newspaper and everything. Can't you just see it? 'Kids Catch Bandit' or 'Girls Grab Green Pillowcase Bandit.'"

But after I'd run out of headlines, I thought, what if Ivy was right? What if the robber completely bypasses Broadhead? Then what will we do? In mystery stories something suspicious always turns up, but where would we find something suspicious in Broadhead?

The Peacock Hotel? No, nobody ever stays there anymore, not since they built the Country Court Motel out by the highway. The bus station? The dime store? Too bad Broadhead didn't have a prison. Then we could have a jail break. Jackson, Michigan has a huge prison. Too bad we didn't live in Jackson. I yawned. Where else? The Wentworth place? I closed my mouth with a snap. The Wentworth place. But now that I'd thought of it, I kind of wished I hadn't. Nobody in their right mind would go there alone. But then I told myself, I wouldn't have to go there alone. Ivy would have to come too. That's what

10

best friends are for. I pulled the sheet up around my neck and wiggled down in the bed. But there was no hurry, I decided. We could save the Wentworth place for the last resort. The very last.

Three

Ivy's Hunch

When Ivy woke up the next morning, I was busy digging through the bottom drawer of my dresser.

"Look at this." I held up a small, brown spiral notebook. "I knew it had to be around somewhere."

Ivy sat up and brushed the hair out of her eyes. "What's it for?"

"For clues!" I could tell Ivy hadn't read very many mysteries. "See, now if the Green Pillowcase Bandit shows up, we'll be all ready for him. We'll use this to keep track of everything he does, and then we'll have all the proof we need for Mr. Bennett and the police."

"But..."

I knew what she was going to say. "And if he doesn't turn up, well, then we'll just have to keep hunting until we find something else to investigate." I liked that word. Investigate.

"Anyway..." I slapped the notebook into the back pocket of my jeans. "We can start at the bank first."

12

"The bank?" Ivy shook her head. "Oh, I don't know, Lizzie. I have a hunch about that place."

"Really? About the Green Pillowcase Bandit?"

"No, uh-uh."

And that was all I could get out of her.

When we went downstairs, Mitch was in the kitchen finishing his breakfast. I decided I was going to ignore him, but he was too busy arguing with Mom to even notice.

"Come on, Mom. It's not fair," he was saying. "How can I ever become a herpetologist if my own family stifles me!"

I didn't bother to listen to the rest of what Mitch said. I'd heard it all before, but I leaned across the table and filled Ivy in as we ate.

"A herpetologist is a person who studies snakes and lizards and things like that," I whispered. "And Mitch and Billy want to buy this great big snake, but Dad said no and Billy's mom said no, so now they're mad at everybody."

"I hardly think you're being stifled," Mom said. "Most of the time your room looks like a branch of the Detroit Zoo. Your dad just said you couldn't bring a wild snake into the house."

The zoo part was true. When Mitch was going to be a zoologist, he had gerbils, rabbits, a three-legged chipmunk that Basil had found, a pair of canaries (they never sang) and Clara. He still has Clara. She's a guinea pig.

The argument ended the way it usually did. If Dad says no, then Mom says no too. Mitch calls them the "United Front."

When Mitch left the kitchen in a huff, Ivy said, "Poor Mitch."

"Poor Mitch!" I couldn't believe it. "How would you like to have a great big slimy snake in your house? Can you imagine if it ever got loose!" Just the thought gave me the shivers. I'm not afraid of spiders or mice or bats or anything like that. Just snakes. My dad is scared of them too. I think it's hereditary.

13

"Snakes aren't slimy," Ivy said. "We learned all about them in science class. Their skin is dry and smooth."

"Ugh, I don't even want to talk about it." I jumped up and started clearing the table. "Besides, why waste time talking about snakes when we could be uptown..." I lowered my voice "...looking for you-know-who."

I thought we were going straight to the bank, but when we got as far as the library, Ivy stopped. "Wait, I promised Chris I'd check in if we came uptown."

Chris is Chris Featherstone. Ivy is the only person I know who calls her father by his first name. He's our librarian. He is also very handsome and has a mustache, and I think he's read every single book in the library.

Broadhead Public Library. No Eating. No Bare Feet, said the sign on the door. I looked down at our bare feet.

"I'll get him," Ivy said. She gave the glass door a push and ducked her head in, keeping her feet out.

"He's at the card catalog," she reported. She pulled her head back just before the door swung closed. She gave it another push. "He's talking to Mrs. Morely." This time she managed to wave at him. "And there's Baby Imogene! She does have more hair."

I took the clue book out of my pocket and started making some notes. You could never tell when something might be important later.

On the first page I wrote *Library. June 20th.* I checked my watch. It was really Mitch's old Boy Scout watch with a new band. *10:10. Mrs. Morely. Baby Imogene.*

I was still writing all this down when Chris Featherstone came out.

"Hi, Lizzie, nice to see you." When he smiled, his brown eyes crinkled up in the corners just like Ivy's. "What have you two been up to this morning?"

"Nothing," we said.

I saw him looking at the clue book, but he didn't ask about it. I knew he wouldn't. He wasn't nosy like some people I know.

I waited while he and Ivy talked about what he was

going to cook for dinner. Ivy is a very fussy eater, so it took a long time. She hates to eat anything squishy.

As he was leaving, Chris said, "Honey, when you set the table tonight, would you please put on a tablecloth? There's one in the hall closet." His eyes crinkled up again. "I want everything to look really nice because we're going to have a special guest for dinner."

"A special guest?" Ivy stared after her father. "I didn't know we were having a special guest."

"Maybe he just invited them," I offered.

Ivy chewed on a strand of hair and didn't answer.

The First National Bank of Broadhead is on the corner of Main and Thomas, right across the street from Chapel of the Chimes Funeral Home. The bank has two big gray columns outside, and inside it always smells of lemon furniture polish and cigars. When I was little, I thought it was Mr. Bennett's house.

I pushed open the heavy door and looked around for Ivy. She was still standing in the middle of the sidewalk.

"Aren't you coming in?"

Ivy hesitated and then spit out the strand of hair. "Okay, but if that EvaLynne Hayes is in there—" Ivy squinted up her eyes and looked mean. "—then I'm coming right back out again."

"EvaLynne? Why? She never babysat for you, did she?"

EvaLynne Hayes babysat for us once when Mom and Dad went to a conference in Dayton, Ohio. It was awful. I guess she'd be all right for little kids, but Mitch and I couldn't stand her. She talked baby talk to us the whole time.

"Ugh, no." Ivy looked shocked. "But this is where she works, isn't it?" When I nodded, she said grimly, "That's what I thought."

The marble floor of the bank was so cold, it made my feet sting. Ivy slipped in and stood right behind me.

"Do you see her?"

"Not yet."

We edged sideways over to the long table where the deposit and withdrawal slips are. There was a line at the teller's widow. Super! Five suspects. But then I realized I knew every single one of them. And two of them were teachers.

Then I spotted someone else. Someone I had never seen before.

"Hey, look over there." I nodded my head toward the man standing near the copy machine. He was tall with red hair. I couldn't see what color his eyes were because he had on those funny black sunglasses that look like mirrors.

"See how he keeps checking his watch," I said. I tried to talk out of the corner of my mouth in case anyone was watching us. "He sure acts jumpy. Look how he keeps snapping and unsnapping the locks on his briefcase. What do you—"

"Look," Ivy said. "There she is."

I turned around. They were changing tellers, and Ivy was right. The new one was EvaLynne Hayes. She had spotted us too. Her curls bounced as she gave a little wave. "See you tonight," she called softly. Ivy cringed as people in line turned to see who she was talking to.

"Quick, let's go." She tugged on my arm.

"No, wait." I wanted to see what the red-haired man was going to do next, but Ivy almost jerked me off my feet. "Lizzie, come *on!*" She pulled me toward the door.

The man was just opening his briefcase as the heavy bank door swung shut behind us.

"Ivy! We didn't even get to see what he had in his briefcase. Maybe it was a gun! Or a bomb!"

I don't think Ivy even heard me. She was sputtering mad. Her bare feet made a slap-slap sound on the sidewalk.

"Special guest, ha!" she said. "I had a hunch something was up. On the way home from the airport we stopped at the library, and there she was! Hanging around the reference desk! And now she's coming for dinner."

Ivy was walking so fast, I had to run to keep up. "But we're always having people over for dinner," I said. I couldn't understand why she was so mad. "It just means

16

that you have more dishes to wash, that's all." Then it sank in. They were having a date. Chris Featherstone and Eva-Lynne Hayes. I didn't even know people that age had dates. I peeked over at Ivy. Her face was still red. Any minute I knew she was going to start chomping on her hair.

I tried to think of something to make her feel better. "Well, at least you're really good at hunches."

"Hunches! Ugh!"

Four

In Disguise

Right after breakfast the next morning I added the rest of yesterday's notes to the clue book.

Bank. June 20th. Tall man with red hair. Mirror sunglasses. Briefcase (with snaps). Acted nervous. I thought a minute and added, *Seen lurking by copy machine.* Lurking. I liked that. Then at the bottom of the page I wrote *Who is he?* in big letters and underlined it.

I wished Ivy hadn't dragged me out of the bank so fast because then we'd probably know the answer. He *could* have just been waiting for somebody, but still.... I chewed on the pencil. He was awfully jumpy. And why would anybody wear those funny sunglasses inside a bank? Unless—I thought of all the TV movies I'd seen—unless he was hiding behind them! I snapped the notebook closed and decided to call Ivy. We had nothing to lose. Besides, he was our only suspect.

I dialed Ivy's number, let it ring three times and then hung up. I counted to ten and dialed again.

Ivy answered on the first ring. "Is that you, Lizzie?"

18

"Ivy! You were supposed to let it ring two more times, remember? That was the signal." But I wasn't really mad. "Listen, I've got an idea. Can you—"

Mitch walked into the kitchen.

"Can I what?" Ivy asked. "What, Lizzie?"

"Ch-tim," I muttered into the phone. "Ch-tim." That was our code name for Mitch last summer. It's *Mitch* sort of spelled backwards.

"Ch—oh!" Ivy remembered.

I waited impatiently while Mitch rummaged through the refrigerator. It took him forever, and after all that, what he took was an egg—a raw egg. I shook my head. Sometimes I really wondered about him.

"He's gone," I said. "Finally. Listen, can you meet me in front of my house at—" I checked my watch. "—at 11:15?" Then I had a brilliant idea. "And Ivy? Wear sunglasses. We've got some investigating to do."

Ivy was exactly on time, but when I saw her coming up the front walk, I groaned.

"What's the matter?" But she knew. She pulled the sunglasses off and stuck them behind her back.

"Did you have to wear pink ones? Pink ones with seashells on the corners?"

I already had on my glasses. I'd found them in the sixty-nine-cent bin in the dime store. They were a little big, but at least they weren't pink.

"These were the only ones I could find," Ivy said. "They were a present from Chris—from Florida."

"Well, okay, but..." I tried to think of a nice way of putting it. "Just don't put them on in the bank unless you have to, all right?"

I started down the walk, but Ivy didn't move. "If you're going to the bank," she said, "forget it. I'm never setting foot in that place again." She jammed her sunglasses back on. "At least not while *she's* there."

EvaLynne Hayes! I'd forgotten all about her. "Did she come for dinner?" I could tell by Ivy's face that she had. "Was it awful?"

Ivy nodded, two hard jerks.

"Well?" I waited. "What happened?"

"She brought me flowers."

I looked at her. "Flowers? What kind of flowers?"

"Just flower flowers." Ivy sounded crabby. "She said they were for the little hostess. Oh, it was awful, Lizzie. She had this big, fakey smile on her face the whole night—even when she was eating. And her perfume! It was so stinky, it made me sneeze."

Poor Ivy. I was afraid to ask if EvaLynne still talked baby talk. "I guess, we don't *have* to go to the bank," I said, hoping she would change her mind, but it didn't work.

She plunked down on the porch steps like a sack of potatoes. "Good."

With a sigh, I put my sunglasses back in my pocket and sat down beside her. Neither one of us said anything. After a minute there was a soft scratching at the front door. I got up and let Basil out. He trotted right over to Ivy, all wiggly-glad to see her, but for once Ivy didn't fuss over him.

"Here, Basil," I called, but instead he disappeared under the front bushes and came back a minute later, proud as punch, with a small rock in his mouth. He dropped it at Ivy's feet and gave a little bark. Even Ivy had to smile at that. Retrieving rocks is one of Basil's favorite games. Plain, ordinary rocks. Mitch says Basil should be in Ripley's *Believe It Or Not,* but then it was Mitch who taught him that trick in the first place.

Ivy couldn't resist. "Okay, Basil, you win." She gave the rock a toss. Basil scrambled after it, his tail waving. He brought it back and barked for more. After a couple more tosses, Ivy looked happier.

"Ivy?" I didn't even have to ask.

"Okay, I'll come, but..." She folded her arms across her chest. "But I won't go into the bank."

"Don't worry, you won't have to," I promised. "You won't even have to be on the same side of the street."

But when I showed Ivy her lookout post, she wasn't very happy. "Here? Right here in front of the *funeral home?*"

"Sure, it's perfect. The bank is right across the street. Besides"—I patted the huge stone pot filled with red geraniums—"you can always pretend you're looking at the flowers."

Ivy rolled her eyes. "Thanks heaps."

I remembered to put on my sunglasses before I stepped into the bank. They made everything so dark, I had to peer over the top of them to see where I was going. I spotted EvaLynne right off. It was a good thing Ivy hadn't come in with me after all. I edged over to the long table and took out a couple of withdrawal slips. While I pretended to fill one out, I took a quick look around. No, no tall red-haired man. Shoot. Somehow I just thought he'd be here. Then I used up four more slips hoping he'd walk through the door, but he didn't. Neither did anyone else. It was definitely a slow day for suspects. I glanced at my watch. I couldn't wait much longer—not with Ivy outside sniffing the flowers. Maybe the red-haired man wasn't mysterious after all. Maybe he was just ordinary. The thought was depressing. Then we'd have to start our search all over again for something suspicious.

I waited five more minutes and then crammed all the withdrawal slips into my pocket and slipped out the door. I looked across the street.

Ivy? For a second I thought she must have gotten tired of waiting and gone home. Then I saw her. At least part of her. She was hunkered down behind the stone flowerpot with only her brown hair and pink sunglasses showing over the tops of the geraniums. Then she saw me too and waved. Her mouth was moving, but I couldn't tell what she was saying.

When I got across the street, she reached out and pulled me down behind the flowers. "Look!" She pointed kitty-corner across the street to the park.

"Look at what?" I took off my sunglasses to see better. "What is it?" The only person I saw was old Mr. Papijac and his dog, Sam.

"There." Ivy pointed again. "Right there."

21

Then I saw him—the red-haired stranger. He was sitting two park benches away from Mr. Papijac, half hidden behind a newspaper.

"I didn't see him at first." Ivy sounded out of breath. "Then I did. I couldn't believe it." Ivy shook my arm as she talked. "Watch, Lizzie. Watch what he does."

I stared so hard, my eyes began to water. Then I saw it too. He slowly, slowly lowered the newspaper and looked across the street at the bank. He still had on those mirror sunglasses. They glinted silver in the sun. There was another flash of silver as he checked his watch. Then he ducked behind the paper again.

"Did you see that?" Ivy said. "What do you think he's doing?"

I couldn't take my eyes off him. "I don't know."

From the bell tower of St. Andrew's Church came twelve slow bongs. Twelve o'clock.

Ivy suddenly gave me a hard poke. EvaLynne Hayes was coming out of the bank. She didn't look our way but headed down Main Street toward the shops.

"Look how she wiggles her bottom," Ivy said. "It's disgusting."

"Ssssssh!"

The mysterious stranger had folded up his newspaper and started down Main Street too. When EvaLynne began to walk a little faster, he began to walk a little faster.

"Hey, maybe he's following her."

EvaLynne never looked back. She walked past Johnson's Drug, past the Red Cross shoe store. She didn't even pause at Leuchtman's bakery.

Ivy let out a yelp. "There's Chris."

He was standing in front of the Stop Inn coffee shop with a big smile on his face. EvaLynne's curls gave a bounce. I just knew she was smiling at him too. He opened the door of the coffee shop, and they went in together.

I turned and looked for the mysterious stranger. "Ivy, where'd he go?" We looked up and down the street, but he had disappeared. Just disappeared.

"Gosh." I sat down on the grass. "What do you think he was doing?"

"Having lunch with EvaLynne behind my back," Ivy snapped.

"No, I mean the other man. The mysterious stranger. There he was sort of hiding behind his newspaper and watching the bank. And then he followed EvaLynne down Main Street and disappeared." My voice rose. "And remember yesterday? Remember how he sort of hid in one corner of the bank near the copy machine? It's almost as if he's waiting or watching for something—or someone."

My own words gave me the shivers. "Oh, Ivy, wouldn't it be great if he was the bank robber? Wow!" I fell back on the grass and stared up at the sky. I felt almost dizzy. "Gosh, if we caught him, Mitch would be so jealous he'd have kittens!" Then I had another thought. "Or maybe he's following EvaLynne because he wants to kidnap her and hold her for ransom."

"Oh, who would pay for her?" Ivy said.

"Well . . ." I couldn't think of a soul.

Ivy gave a sniff as if to say I-told-you-so.

"Well, he *could* be a kidnapper," I said. I hated to give up on the idea. "Maybe she's really rich and we just don't know it." I searched through my pockets and pulled out an unused withdrawal slip. "Anyway, we can warn her and the bank at the same time." I chewed on the top of my pencil. "What do you think we should say?"

"Leave Chris Featherstone alone or else!"

"Oh, we can't say that. She'd know right off it was us. What about . . ." I thought a minute and wrote, DANGER. YOU ARE BEING FOLLOWED. MAY BE G.P.B. I remembered to print the words in big crooked letters in case anyone tried to trace the handwriting. I signed it, A FRIEND.

Ivy looked over my shoulder and made a face at the signature. Then she put her finger on the initials.

"The Green Pillowcase Bandit," I explained. "I sort of ran out of room, but she should be able to figure that out."

Ivy gave another sniff. "I doubt it."

I ran across the street and left the note on the long table, face down with the words EVALYNNE HAYES. PERSONAL! printed on the top.

Ivy was waiting at the corner when I came out. Without a word, we started to run. We ran and ran until my side ached and I had to slow down.

"What do you think she'll do when she reads it?" I asked.

"I don't know. Maybe she'll get scared and run away." For the first time all day, Ivy sounded almost cheerful.

Five

Something Odd About Mitch

"When did you first notice something odd about the so-called mysterious stranger?" asked Suzanne Small from NBC News.

I tried to look modest. "Well, actually from the very beginning Ivy Frances Featherstone and I—"

"Have you noticed anything odd lately about Mitch?" Mom asked.

"Mitch?" I blinked and Suzanne Small disappeared. "What do you mean, *lately?* If you ask me, there's always been something a little odd about him."

"Lizzie." Dad looked at me over the top of his glasses.

Dad, Mom and I were just finishing breakfast. Saturdays around our house are pretty much like the other days of the week because Dad has office hours from nine to four. He's a dentist. Mom used to go to work with him. She kept the office books after Miss Murphy left to get married. That was after she'd given up real estate and before she'd gone back to college, but it didn't work out. I guess there are lots of different ways of keeping books because one day Mom came home and announced that she'd retired, but I think Dad sort of fired her. Mitch and I were glad. As soon as they stopped working together, they stopped fighting and went back to being the "United Front" again.

"What's the matter with Mitch?" I reached for more toast.

"I don't know exactly. It's like he's never home even when he is home. Do you know what I mean?"

I nodded, but I wasn't sure I did. When Mitch came thudding down the back stairs, he seemed just the same to me.

"I don't have time for eggs," he said. "I'm late already." His hair was wet and slicked back from the shower. "I've got three lawns to mow before lunch."

"You're sure busy this summer," Mom said. "Seems like you're never home anymore."

"Just love to work, I guess." Mitch poured himself a glass of orange juice and then reached across the table and stole a piece of toast off my plate.

For once I didn't holler at him. I was too surprised. Mitch in love with work? Since when?

Mom squinched up her eyes and looked at him as if she was trying to see inside his head. I could tell she was having a hard time swallowing that one too.

"What are you going to do with all your money?" I asked when the phone rang.

"I'll get it! It's Ivy." I jumped up. Maybe something had happened about EvaLynne and our note already. But Mitch got to the phone first.

"Yeah, hi." He hunched his shoulders around the receiver and lowered his voice. "Yep, everything's fine."

I sank back down in my chair. I bet he was talking to old Peabrain.

"Tomorrow?" Mitch asked. "I don't know."

I stopped chewing to listen. If he was going anyplace fun tomorrow, I wanted to go too.

"How much?" Mitch shook his head. "No, too expensive.

Hmmmm. Toro would really like that." His voice went even lower. "It would be sort of risky, but maybe. Yeah, maybe."

Too expensive? Sort of risky? What was Mitch talking about?

"That was a strange conversation," Mom said after he'd hung up.

"Yeah," I said. "Who's Toro?"

Mitch got a funny look on his face. "Just a friend," he said. Then he laughed. "Yep, good old Sam Toro." He squeezed out the back door and stepped over Basil. "You'd love him, Lizzie," he called back through the screen.

I snorted. That would be the day when I loved any dumb friend of his.

When the phone rang again two seconds later, it was finally for me. "Lizzie? This is Ivy Featherstone." No matter how many times a day Ivy calls, she always says, "This is Ivy Featherstone." "Have you heard anything about the you-know-what we wrote to you-know-who?"

I could tell that Chris hadn't left for work yet either. Just like Dad, he has to work on Saturdays.

"No, have you?"

"No." Her voice was glum. "But I think they have another date tonight. Chris whistled all through breakfast."

Poor Ivy. "Can you come over..." I was about to say "now," but Mom shook her head at me.

"I need your help cleaning out the storage room this morning," she said.

"...er...can you come over after lunch?" I asked Ivy.

"Okay." Her voice sounded a little brighter. "What are we going to do?"

"I don't know, but we'll think of something."

Cleaning out the basement storage room wasn't so bad. It was mostly filled with newspapers and about ninety million old *Time* magazines. Dad hates to throw anything out. We were stacking the newspapers into boxes for the Lion's Club paper drive when I found Mitch's old Boy Scout whistle among the piles. I couldn't believe the sound it made. Neither could Mom. She jumped about three feet.

"Gosh, it sounds just like a police whistle, doesn't it?"

"Yes, it does," Mom said in a steely voice. "And I wouldn't recommend blowing it in this house again. Ever!"

I showed the whistle to Ivy first thing when she came over after lunch. We were upstairs in my room with the door closed behind us. "Basil, move your nose so Ivy can see." He had followed us up the stairs.

"Don't blow it or Mom will kill me," I warned her. "It's so loud, it will take the roof off."

"Did it really belong to Mitch?" Ivy touched it gently with one finger. "Can I hold it?"

"Sure." I dropped it into her hands and then pulled out the clue book from my bottom drawer.

The trouble was that after Ivy and I had taken turns writing down everything that had happened yesterday—the mysterious stranger in the park, EvaLynne, and our note—we were stuck. What should we do next?

"Do you want another cookie?" I looked into the bag of chocolate chip cookies I'd brought up with us. There was only one left. Basil pricked up his ears. "No, you've already had three," I told him.

Ivy shook her head. "It's too hot to eat."

It was never too hot for me. Besides, I hated to see a good cookie go to waste. I ate it in two bites and then licked my fingers.

"Too bad it's Saturday and the bank's closed," I said. "Even if we went uptown, we wouldn't know where to look for him."

Ivy yawned. "Maybe he's over at EvaLynne's."

"Do you really think so!"

"No." Ivy looked startled. "I was just kidding."

"But he might be. Maybe he's going to kidnap her and hold her hostage until Mr. Bennett gives him all the bank's money."

Ivy sniffed, but I really liked the idea. "Come on, Ivy. It'll be easy. We'll just go by and make sure everything's all right. EvaLynne won't even know we're around."

"Yes, but what if she does see us? Then what?" Ivy frowned. "Besides, we don't even know where she lives."

I could tell she was weakening. "That won't be hard to find out. She's probably in the phone book."

And she was. "901 North Palmer," I read out loud. "That's not even very far from here. Now all we need is some kind of disguise. Too bad it's not raining. Then we could use Mom's umbrella."

The cookie bag crinkled. I turned around. Basil was trying to lick the crumbs from the bottom of the bag.

"Aha! He can be our cover. That way everyone will think we're just two girls out walking our dog."

"I don't know," Ivy muttered. "He doesn't cover enough of us to do much good." That made both of us giggle.

When we got to the corner of North Palmer and Pike, Ivy wouldn't go any closer. "I'll be the lookout again," she said. She stationed herself by the big mailbox while Basil and I started down the street.

Since Basil had to sniff every single tree, I had plenty of time to look around. Even before I saw 901, I knew it had to be the right house. It was a small pretty white one with a green porch. Pasted on the mailbox and on the screen door were big, yellow smiley faces that said, Have a Good Day! The only person I saw, though, was a bald-headed man washing his car a couple of houses down. I was really disappointed. No mysterious stranger. And no EvaLynne.

"But she must be home," I reported back to Ivy. "Her front door's open." I pointed to the big brown Cadillac parked across the street. "Doesn't that look sort of familiar?"

Ivy shook her head. "Not to me."

I was sure I'd seen it before, but I couldn't remember where. I shrugged. It probably didn't matter. "Let's sneak around to the back and see if we can see anything there."

"Lizzie, we can't do that!"

"Sure we can."

EvaLynne's alley looked just like the one behind my house—full of weeds and garbage cans.

"Come on, nobody will care," I said when Ivy hesitated, but I wasn't really so sure that was true. Delight Nelson was always threatening to call the police when she saw strange kids in our alley. "We'll take a quick look around and then leave," I promised.

Basil was in dog heaven. He wanted to stop and sniff every smelly garbage can. "Ugh, you're disgusting," I told him.

It wasn't hard to find a place to hide behind EvaLynne's house. There was a row of thick bushes down the back of her fence. We crawled along pulling Basil behind us until we found a hole in the bushes to peep through. There wasn't much to see after all. EvaLynne's backyard looked just like her front one—just grass and some rosebushes.

Ivy pulled on my sleeve. "Let's go."

That's when the back screen door opened. Ivy let out a squeak. It was EvaLynne. She was all dressed up in a blue flowered dress and blue shoes. Even her eyelids were blue.

We both froze. From inside the house came a deep voice. A man's voice. I couldn't hear what he said.

"Your iced tea is on the counter," EvaLynne called back.

"Maybe it's the mysterious stranger," I whispered.

"I hope it's not Chris."

"It's delicious!" the man said. He gave the screen door a push and stepped outside. It was Mr. Wendell Bennett.

"Oh!" I couldn't believe it.

"Who's that?" Ivy whispered. But Basil recognized his friend right away. He gave a leap that would have pulled us clear through the fence if I hadn't jerked back on the leash.

"Run!" Keeping our heads down we backed out of the bushes and started running down the alley, dragging Basil behind us.

We didn't slow down or look back until we were almost home.

"Who was that?" Ivy demanded.

"That was Mr. Bennett," I said. When Ivy didn't say anything, I added, "He's the president of the bank." Then I re-membered the car. "That's why the car looked so familiar. It was his. But why would he be visiting EvaLynne? And on a Saturday?" Then I knew. "The note!" I groaned. "She must have told him about the note we wrote."

"But that's good," Ivy said. "Then he'll know all about the mysterious stranger and be looking out for him."

"I guess so," I said slowly. "I just hope they don't know that *we* wrote it or they'll be looking out for *us!*"

Six

Mitch?

"Did you hear about the store in Detroit that was robbed five times in one year?" Mitch asked.

Sunday lunch was over but we were still sitting around the table. I was counting up the plates. It was my turn to do the dishes.

Mitch didn't wait for an answer. "Well, the owner got so fed up, he went out and bought a pair of six-foot bull snakes. Six feet long *each!* Then he turned them loose in the store every night and put up this big sign: Beware of Giant Snakes!"

Mom and Dad looked at each other. Mitch never gives up when he wants something.

"What happened next?" I asked in spite of myself.

Mitch grinned. "Nothing. Absolutely nothing. That's the whole point of the story. Everyone was so scared of bumping into the snakes in the dark that the man hasn't been robbed since. Isn't that a great idea?"

"Ugh, no." Just the thought of stepping on any snake

made my skin crawl, let alone stepping on one that was six feet long.

I could tell by Dad's face that he didn't think giant snakes were great either. "That's very interesting, Mitch," he said, "but I still don't want a snake in the house."

"It wouldn't have to be *in* the house," Mitch said. "Billy and I could build a cage for it in the garage and—"

I tuned out the rest of the argument and started clearing the table. I kept thinking about yesterday. I sure hoped EvaLynne hadn't seen us. And it would be even worse if Mr. Bennett had. He might tell Dad that Ivy and I were snooping around, and that would mean the end of all our investigating for the entire summer.

Mitch wandered into the kitchen before I finished the dishes. He took an apple out of the wooden bowl and polished it against his shirt.

"Lizzie?"

"What?"

"Ah . . . nothing."

I turned around and looked at him.

"No, never mind," he said.

If there is one thing that drives me wild, it's for someone to start to say something and then say "never mind."

"What?" I said.

"Hush, both of you," Mom called from the dining room. "I'm working on a paper."

Now that Mom is in college, it seems as if she always has some kind of paper to write. I asked her once what she was going to be when she finally graduates, and she said, "Tired."

"What were you going to say," I demanded in a whisper.

"I said," he whispered back, "never mind!"

Ivy called. In fact, she called twice, once right after the other. She called the first time to tell me that her hunch had been right again. Chris had had a date with EvaLynne last night, only Ivy had been invited too. "We went to the movies and EvaLynne giggled through the whole thing.

33

'He-he-he'—you should have heard her." Ivy sounded disgusted.

Two seconds later she called back to tell me the good part. EvaLynne hadn't said a word about yesterday. At least not in front of her. That made me feel a whole lot better. Maybe EvaLynne hadn't seen us after all.

When I went into the living room, Dad was there reading the Sunday paper. He had on the blue shirt Mitch and I had given him for his birthday. Even if he did wear glasses and didn't have a mustache, he was still handsome. I thought of Ivy and wondered how I'd feel if EvaLynne started coming over here and acting all giggly.

Dad glanced up. "What are you glaring about, Lizzie?"

"Nothing." But then, because I hate it when people say that to me, I added, "I'm just glad you're not single like some people I know."

He looked surprised. Then he grinned. "Well, I hadn't thought about it for a while, but I'm glad I'm not single either."

Mitch came into the living room and settled down on the couch with the sports section. Basil came slinking in after him. Basil wasn't supposed to be in the living room at all, but he curled up small beside the couch and pretended he wasn't there. Dad pretended he hadn't seen him.

"Comics?" he asked.

I started to nod but then changed my mind. "Can I have the front section instead?" I decided if Ivy and I were going to catch the Green Pillowcase Bandit, I'd better keep up with the news.

"Good for you, Lizzie." Dad handed me the newspaper. "I'm glad to see you taking an interest in the larger world around you."

Dad was so pleased, I was embarrassed. I could see Mitch looking at me out of the corner of his eye as I skimmed the headlines. Nothing. At least nothing I was interested in, but now I *had* to read something; so I read about a little girl who had been raised in a chicken coop, and instead of talking, she clucked. It was very interesting and I thought maybe Dad was right. Maybe I should read more about the world around me.

I was about to hand the newspaper back when I noticed an article on the bottom of the last page.

"Look, here's something about the Wentworth place."

Mitch's head jerked up. "What? What does it say?"

"Well, just a second." Taking my time, I ruffled up the newspaper and cleared my throat. "'House haunted by sighs of its past,'" I read out loud.

Dad groaned. "'Haunted by sighs.' That's terrible."

But I liked it. "No, listen: 'Built by Ansell Wentworth for his bride in 1906, the Wentworth place was the pride of Broadhead. But such happiness was not to last. Shortly after the couple's honeymoon trip to Europe, the lovely Mrs. Wentworth died under tragic circumstances.'"

"Gosh." I stopped reading. "Tragic circumstances!"

Dad snorted, but at least Mitch was taking it seriously.

"'Broken hearted, Ansell Wentworth abandoned his magnificent home, never to return. Now the once-proud house has fallen into ruin and is haunted only by sighs of its past.' Then it says that next Sunday they're going to write about the Robert Simpson house which is now Terri's House of Beauty."

"But is that all they say about the Wentworth place?" Mitch asked.

"Uh-huh, except for the picture." The photograph was old and sort of blurry, but it showed how beautiful the house once was with its peaked roof and great round tower over the porch.

"I wonder how Mrs. Wentworth died?" I thought of all the stories I'd heard about that place—and I'd heard a lot—but I'd never heard one about Mrs. Wentworth. "Do you think she was murdered?"

Dad shook his head. "I wouldn't be surprised if the reporter made up that story on the spot to fill the page. Mrs. Wentworth—if there was one—probably died in bed of old age."

I wasn't so sure. I remembered last summer when Mitch

and I had ridden our bikes by the house on the old Green Hills highway. I thought of the tall black iron fence, the boarded-up windows, the sagging roof. No, I shook my head. No, the Wentworth place looked like a place where anything could happen.

Ivy called again just before bedtime. "Fifteen minutes," Mom said when the phone rang. It took a little longer than that, but we finally decided on a plan for tomorrow. This time, if the mysterious stranger showed up, we were going to be ready for him.

"Ready, ready, ready," I sang to the bathroom mirror as I washed my face. "We're ready, ready, ready."

"Lizzie?"

I stopped singing and opened the door a crack. It was Mitch. "I just got in here," I said.

"I know. I wanted to talk to you, that's all."

"You do?" I opened the door a little wider. "About what?"

"I was wondering...er..." Mitch looked a little embarrassed. "I was wondering if I could borrow some money. Just ten dollars or so."

Ten dollars! I stared at him. Here he was with at least fifty million yard jobs, and he wanted to borrow money from me? And ten whole dollars!

"Ah, come on, Lizzie-beth. You know I'll pay you back."

Mitch always calls me Lizzie-beth when he wants something. Like last month when his bike had a flat, he talked me into lending him mine. I didn't care until I found out where he went. He and Peabrain went to the Broadhead Fair and didn't even ask me if I wanted to go.

Just thinking about that made me mad all over again. "What do you need it for?" I demanded.

"I just need it, that's all." He straightened up. "I said I'd pay it back. Now are you going to lend it to me or not?"

If he had been nicer, I'd have been nicer too, but he wasn't, so I wasn't.

"No," I said and closed the door.

But after I had turned off the lights and gotten into bed, I began to wish I hadn't gotten so mad. I did have the money

—well, eight dollars and twenty-eight cents worth—hidden in the Earl Grey tea tin in my bottom drawer. I was saving up for a pair of binoculars, but I could have lent it to Mitch for a little while. I knew he'd pay it back.

Then I began to think about all the nice things he had done for me. Like the time I had the mumps in the second grade and Mitch had spent one whole afternoon reading the Frog and Toad books out loud to me. And the time he punched Giles Norton in the stomach for calling me tubby. And how he always lets me play with Clara, his guinea pig, even though he did buy her with all his own money.

I sighed and got out of bed. The hallway was dark, but there was a strip of light under Mitch's door. Good, he hadn't gone to bed yet.

I tiptoed across the hall. "Mitch?" I could hear his radio playing. "Mitch?"

I opened the door a crack and peeked in. "Pssst, Mitch?" The lights were on, the radio was on, but the room was empty. I turned around, almost expecting to see him behind me. The hallway was silent. The bathroom? But the bathroom was empty too.

Where was he? I crept over to the top of the back stairs and looked down. The kitchen was dark.

"Pssssst, Mitch?"

No answer.

Maybe he was in the living room. I tiptoed back the length of the hallway and hung over the top of the front stairs. I could hear Dad's voice, then Mom's. They were laughing about something. I tiptoed down the stairs and peeked around the posts. No Mitch.

Slowly I crept up the stairs and back into bed. Even though it was warm, I pulled the sheet up to my chin. Where was he? I stared out into the darkness. Where could he have gone?

Seven

The Stakeout

Should I tell or shouldn't I? I didn't know what to do. I was sure—pretty sure—that Mitch had just sneaked off somewhere with Peabrain, but still...maybe I should go tell Mom. I started to get out of bed and then changed my mind. No, I'd better not. If I tattled, Mitch would never speak to me again. Ever.

I closed my eyes, but I couldn't sleep. I kept listening for Mitch. It wasn't fair. Here I was stuck in bed like a baby while he and Billy were out having a great time. They were probably at the Burger Palace or the Dairy Queen this very minute. No, wait. I suddenly remembered that Mitch didn't have any money—or at least not much if he tried to borrow money from me. Then where could he be? What if....I started thinking of all the terrible things that could have happened to him.

What if he'd been hit by a car? Or a truck out of control? That had happened to Toby Martins, a little first grader. The whole school had gone to his funeral. A tear rolled down my cheek. It had been so sad. All the kids cried, even the seventh graders. If anything like that happened to Mitch...my own brother. I could just see us all at his funeral—Mom, Dad and me. And everybody would say, "Lizzie Bruce is the bravest girl I've ever seen. Such a comfort to her parents." I cried harder. Now I wished I'd lent Mitch the money. How could I ever have been so mean? If Mitch comes home, I'll never be mean to him again, I promised. I hiccuped mid-sob and almost smiled. I sounded just like Scarlett O'Hara.

The first sound I heard was Basil barking. I jerked awake and reached for my watch before I realized that it wasn't lamp light but sunlight in my eyes. It was morning.

Mitch? I jumped out of bed and ran across the hall. I knocked once and opened the door. Mitch's bed was torn apart and there were clothes all over the floor. What a relief. He had come home last night after all. But where had he been?

I pulled on yesterday's clothes and took the back stairs two at a time to find out.

"Mom, have you seen—" As I rounded the bottom of the stairs, I saw him myself. There was Mitch, big as life, clamly wolfing down a stack of french toast at the breakfast table.

"Have I seen what?" Mom asked.

"Nobody. I mean, nothing. I mean, it's okay."

Mom gave me one of her long looks. "Well, I hope so."

As soon as the last piece of french toast disappeared, Mitch stood up. "I have to cut Mrs. Lorenzo's grass this morning and clear out her eaves. I might be late for lunch."

"Ooops, I have to meet Ivy," I said. I stood up too. I wasn't about to let him get away that easily.

"Lizzie, this is your week to do the breakfast dishes," Mom began, but I was already following Mitch out the back door. "I can't now, Mom," I called back, "but I'll do them as soon as I get back, promise."

"Mitch? Hey, wait." I caught up with him by the lilac bush and snagged the back of his shirt. "Where were you last night?"

39

"Me?" He tried to look innocent.

"Come on, Mitch. I know you were out somewhere. And . . . and I think that was mean! You didn't even ask me if I wanted to go!"

Mitch sort of choked as if I'd said something funny.

"Where'd you go? Come on, tell me!"

When he shook his head, I got mad. Here I'd been crying my eyes out thinking he was dead or something and he wouldn't even tell me where he'd been.

"I bet you were with that dumb Peabrain and . . . and Sam Toro!" I just made up the part about Sam Toro, but Mitch suddenly stopped laughing, so I knew I'd hit on something. "And just who is this Sam Toro?" I demanded. "Another one of your zero friends?"

"That's for me to know and you to find out, Lizard." Mitch jerked his shirt out of my hand.

Lizard! That really made me mad. "Okay, I will," I said. "I'll find out and then I'll—" Mitch stalked off. "—and then I'll tell the whole world!" I yelled after him.

The bells of St. Andrew's Church started to strike. . . . Seven . . . eight . . . nine. Nine o'clock. Darn, I was late. Ivy would be starting the stakeout without me and all because of Mitch.

It was seventeen minutes after nine and I was running up Main Street when I heard, "Pssst, Lizzie."

I twisted around.

"Psssst, in here."

I peeked into the doorway of the Purple Tree Restaurant. A hand flicked out from the other side of the cigarette machine. It was Ivy's.

"What are you doing here?" I said. "I thought we were supposed to meet next door at Chapel of the Chimes?"

"I know, but somebody stole our spot."

I ducked my head out the doorway. Ivy was right. A large white panel truck was parked right in front of the cement flower pot. We'd need x-ray eyes to see through it. On the side of the truck in small black letters was a name: Penguin Refrigeration.

40

"But look, I found an even better spot." Ivy disappeared inside the restaurant. I sort of tiptoed after her. I hardly ever go into the Purple Tree. For one thing, it's really expensive and for another, the owner, Mr. Tilslit, doesn't like kids. Today most of the booths were empty. I guess it was too late for breakfast and still too early for lunch.

"See." Ivy led me to the front booth. "All we have to do is lean against the window a little and we can still see the bank."

I pushed my forehead against the glass. Perfect. No one could go in or out of the bank without our seeing them. Now the only problem was money. Even after Ivy and I emptied our pockets, we only had enough for two small Cokes. Ivy poked me when I took a big swallow of mine.

"You have to make it last, remember."

"Oh, I bet we see you-know-who sneaking into the bank any minute."

"Who? Chris?"

"No, not him. The mysterious stranger!"

But even taking tiny, tiny sips, we finally finished our Cokes, and we still hadn't seen anything suspicious. We saw lots of people going in and out of the bank, but not *the* person.

"What are we going to do if we do see him?" Ivy asked.

I pulled out the clue book. "First we watch everything he does, and then we write it all down. You know, like what kind of clothes he's wearing and who he's talking to and just everything."

"Then what?" Ivy persisted.

"Well...." Sometimes I wished Ivy wouldn't ask so many questions, especially when I didn't know all the answers. "Well, in a stakeout, you just never know," I told her. "Anything can happen."

"What will it be this time, girls?" The waitress had sneaked up on us in her rubber-soled shoes. She flicked her damp cloth across the table and then stood breathing over us.

I rubbed my wet elbow. "Ah...." I looked at Ivy for help.

"May we have two glasses of water, please?" Ivy asked in a small voice. "We're awfully thirsty."

"Humph, kids!" The waitress came back and set the glasses down with a thunk that made us both jump.

"I sure wish the mysterious stranger would hurry and show up," Ivy whispered. "We can't stay here much longer." Then she straightened up. "Hey, isn't that Mitch? And who's that with him? Billy Hunt?"

"Where?" I bumped my nose against the glass.

"They went into Jake's." She pointed across the street to the pet shop.

"It couldn't be Mitch," I said. "He's cutting Mrs. Lorenzo's grass."

But a few minutes later I saw Billy coming out of the pet shop, and right beside him was Mitch. "Yep, that's Pea-brain, all right. But what do you think *that* is?" They were each carrying one end of a large, rectangular package wrapped in brown paper.

"An aquarium," Ivy said promptly. "It's the right shape."

I shook my head. "Couldn't be. Mitch doesn't have any fish."

"Maybe Billy does."

"Maybe." Then another thought struck me. "I wonder where he got the money."

Ivy was still watching Mitch with that drippy expression on her face. "Probably from all his lawn jobs. Poor Mitch. He works so hard."

"But last night...." I stopped. Last night Mitch wanted to borrow money from me. If he hadn't had enough money last night, where had he gotten it today? It couldn't have been from Billy because Billy was always broke. From that Sam Toro? Could he be the one?

"Lizzie?" Ivy poked me. "Don't look now, but the waitress is staring at us. I think we'd better get out of here."

I did look. And she was. We slid out of the booth and scuttled past her. "Thank you," I whispered.

I'd forgotten how hot it was outside. It was like stepping into an oven.

"Phew!" Ivy lifted her hair off her neck and held it up on top of her head. "Now what are we going to do?"

I looked at my watch. It was only five minutes past eleven. The white truck was still parked in front of our spot. "Well, we could check out the Peacock Hotel. Or the bus station. Maybe he doesn't have a car."

"Which is closest?"

"The bus station."

The bus station smelled of gasoline and old cigar smoke. And it was empty except for Everett who runs the newspaper stand.

"Looking for somebody, girls?" He moved his cigar from one side of his mouth to the other.

"No," said Ivy.

"Yes," I said at the same time.

He looked at us. "Well, which is it?"

"Ah . . . we're looking for a bus schedule," I said quickly.

"Where to? Detroit? Chicago? Ann Arbor? Grand Rapids? Kalamazoo?" He said the names so fast, they sounded like one long word.

"Ah . . ." I didn't know what to do next, but Everett made the decision for us. "Now, go on, Lizzie." He impatiently shooed us toward the door. "You know your dad wouldn't want you hanging around here. Take your little friend and go play somewhere else."

"Playing! We're not playing!" But I said that to Ivy, not to Everett, as we walked back to Main Street. "Darn." I tried to think of where else we could look for him. "We could go to the post office and see if he's on any of the WANTED posters. It's on the way to the hotel."

Ivy sighed. "Okay."

As we passed the bank, I peeked in just to make sure nothing had happened while we were gone. EvaLynne looked up from the teller's window and spotted me.

"Ooooops!" I pulled my head back out. "Nothing," I told Ivy. "He wasn't there."

We stopped at the corner, waiting for the light to change. "I wouldn't mind being that little penguin right now." I pointed across the street to the drawing painted on the door of the white panel truck. It was of a black and white penguin sitting on a block of ice.

Ivy fanned herself with her hand. "In Chicago when it's this hot, the police open up the fire hydrants for the kids. I wish they'd do that here. Oh, there's Mr. Papijac with his dog again. Does he spend every day in the park?"

I didn't answer. For the first time I noticed that there was somebody in the truck. A man. He had on a kind of uniform—a green hat and a long-sleeved shirt. It was hard to see his face because he had sunglasses on. Dark, mirror sunglasses.

As I watched, the man pulled off his hat and wiped his forehead with his sleeve. His hair glinted red in the sunlight.

"Ivy!"

Almost as if he'd heard me, the man turned and stared straight at me. I didn't move. Then he reached down and started the motor of the truck.

"Ivy, that's him!"

She jerked around. "Who? Where?" I pointed, but it was too late. He had pulled past us. The red brake lights on the truck glowed as he slowed down to turn the corner and then he was gone.

"That was him," I said. "The mysterious stranger! He was right there in the truck the whole time." My voice cracked. "We were staking out a stakeout. A real one. And we didn't even know it!"

Eight

It's for You

"Are you sure it was him?" Ivy stared at me.

I nodded slowly. "I'm positive. He was right there in that truck. Right there in front of us."

"Maybe he was just waiting for somebody..." Her voice trailed off. I knew she was thinking of EvaLynne. "Or maybe it wasn't him after all. Maybe it was somebody that just looked like him."

"Ivy, it *was* him! He had on the same sunglasses and everything. And he was doing just what he was doing last time—watching the bank."

"But why would anybody do that unless...unless he really was...oh, Lizzie, you don't really think he could be the Green Pillowcase Bandit, do you? I mean, he couldn't *really* be, could he?"

Could he? All along it had been fun thinking he might be, but now...now this wasn't fun any more.

"Let's go home," Ivy said as if she could tell what I was thinking.

45

"Okay." Then I stopped. "No, wait. We have to warn the bank first."

I ripped a piece of paper out of the clue book and scribbled EvaLynne's name on the front. This time I didn't have to worry about disguising my handwriting. It was so jerky and crooked that even I wouldn't recognize it.

On the back I wrote: BEWARE OF THE MAN IN THE WHITE PENGWUIN TRUCK.

"How do you spell *penguin?*"

"It doesn't matter," Ivy said. "Just hurry."

The marble floor of the bank was cold and slick as ice. I slapped the note face down on the long table and ran right back out again.

Ivy was waiting for me. She grabbed me by the hand and pulled me along. "Did she see you? Was she there?" She kept hold of my hand so I wouldn't slow down.

"Uh-huh, she was there. I saw her. Now I just hope she sees the note." A sudden thought jerked me to a stop.

"What's the matter?"

"I just thought of something." I swallowed. "What if he's been there *every* day and we just haven't seen him before."

"Lizzie, don't say that! I bet you made a mistake. Lots of people wear sunglasses and have red hair."

"No, it was him all right," I said. "I know it was. I looked right at him and..." I snapped my mouth shut, suddenly remembering that he had looked right back at me too.

Mom was weeding the marigolds in the front yard when we came up the walk. Just seeing her made me feel better. It was going to be all right now. Mom would know what to do.

"Mom! Guess what happened? I mean, what I think happened. Ivy and I—"

"Elizabeth Mary Bruce." Mom stood up and slapped the dirt off her hands. "I have just finished the breakfast dishes, the dishes you were supposed to do this morning."

"Excuse me," Ivy whispered. "I think I have to use the bathroom."

The dishes! I'd forgotten all about them, but Mom hadn't.

She was mad at Mitch too. He hadn't weeded the marigolds or clipped the grass along the fence.

"I just told Mitch and now I'm telling you, Lizzie. This is not a hotel. We all live here, and we all have to share the work."

I saw Ivy's face at the screen door waiting for me. It disappeared again as Mom said, "You and Mitch are expected to do your chores first and then play with your friends."

"But we weren't playing. We—"

"Elizabeth?" Mom fixed her eyes on me. There was only one answer.

"Yes, Mother."

I was halfway up the stairs to find Ivy when Mom called through the screen. "Oh, I forgot. Someone called about five minutes ago."

I stopped. "For me?" Nobody ever called me except Ivy. "Who was it?"

"I don't know. Mitch took the message. Said they'd call back."

I took two more steps and froze. I had an awful thought. A really awful thought. "Mom? Was it a man?"

"I don't know." Her voice was fainter. "Ask Mitch."

"Where is he? Mitch, I mean?"

No answer.

I crept up the stairs and knocked softly on Mitch's door. "Mitch?"

No answer there either. I leaned against the wall trying to think. It couldn't have been the mysterious stranger. It couldn't have been him—could it? Could he have been watching us the whole time we were watching him? And I know he saw me today. He looked straight at me. It would have been easy for him to find out who I was. Broadhead is so small that all he'd have to do is ask and someone would be sure to say, "Oh, you mean Dr. Bruce's daughter? Blond and sort of big for her age?"

I groaned out loud.

"Lizzie?" Ivy poked her head out of my bedroom door.

"What are you doing out there? What's wrong? What did your mom say?"

"She was so mad I didn't get a chance to tell her anything. But now something even worse has happened." I followed her into my room and closed the door. "Now, I don't *know* it was him. It could have been anyone but..." Then I told her about the phone call.

"Quick!" Ivy slid off the bed and stood up. "Let's go tell your mom. She'll know—"

Brrrrrrrrrrring! Brrrrrrrrring!

It was the phone. I sat stone still.

"I'll answer it," Ivy said. "I'll say I've never heard of you."

"No, wait. Maybe he'll give up."

Brrrrrring! Brrrrr—

The ringing stopped. I let out my breath. He had given up.

"Lizzie?" It was Mom's voice. She sounded as if she was standing at the foot of the stairs. "Telephone, honey. It's for you."

Ivy and I looked at each other. "It's him," I said. "I just know it."

"Liz?" Mom sounded impatient. "Are you coming? I have to move the sprinkler. Water's coming in the windows." Her voice faded away.

"I'll go with you," Ivy whispered. "And if it's him, just hang up. Then we'll run and get your mom, okay?"

I swallowed and nodded. "Okay." We went down the back stairs and into the kitchen. I was glad Ivy was with me. The receiver was lying on the counter. I picked it up with two fingers and held it away from my ear.

"Hello?"

"Hello?" The voice was very faint. "Hello?"

"What's he saying?" Ivy demanded. She was standing so close, her hair tickled my bare arm.

"I don't know." I brought the receiver closer to my ear. "Hello?" I said again.

"Lizzie? This is Mrs. Morely. Can you and Ivy babysit for

Imogene tomorrow afternoon? Say about two o'clock? You can tell your mom I'll only be gone an hour or so."

"Oh, yes!" I said. "I'm sure we can."

Ivy grabbed my arm. "Don't talk to him. Hang up!"

"I'll ask my mom and call you back," I said quickly. "Good—"

Ivy yanked the phone out of my hand and hung up. "You weren't supposed to talk to him. You were supposed to hang up!"

"No, it's okay." I felt like dancing around the kitchen. "It wasn't him. It was Mrs. Morely!" I started to giggle. "She wants us to babysit tomorrow."

"Mrs. Morely?" Ivy's voice went high and squeaky. "Baby Imogene's mother? And we thought . . . Oh gosh, and I hung up on her!"

That only made me laugh harder.

Brrrrrrrrrring! Brrrrrrrrring!

I jumped at the sound. Ivy's giggle turned into a hiccup.

Slowly I walked over to the phone and picked it up. "Hello?"

"Hello? Lizzie?" It was a man's voice. I almost dropped the phone. "May I please speak to Ivy. This is Chris Featherstone."

Oh, boy. I passed the phone to Ivy. "It's your father," I mouthed.

Ivy didn't say much. A couple of *yes*'s and *okay*'s. When she hung up, her face was white.

"That was Chris," she said as if I didn't know. "He said he'd like both of us to come down and see him." She twisted a long strand of hair around her finger. "And Lizzie? He sounded kind of mad."

Nine

Trying to Explain

"You don't think your dad is really, really mad, do you?" It had been a long, hot walk uptown, but now, standing in front of the library, neither one of us was in any hurry to go in.

"He never gets *really* mad." Ivy dug at the crabgrass growing between the sidewalk squares with the heel of her sandal. "Well, hardly ever."

"Oh." That made me feel even worse.

"I guess your mom's sort of mad at us too, huh?"

"Sort of. I'll probably be doing dishes every day for the next five years," I said glumly. But right now I was more worried about Ivy's father than my mom. "Are you sure he didn't say anything else when he called?"

"Nope, he just said he wanted to talk to us. Both of us. But I bet that EvaLynne tattled on us." She squinted up her eyes. "I bet she figured out who wrote the notes and then ran and told Chris. Boy, that's what we get for watching out for her and her dumb bank!" She brushed her hair off her face and hooked it behind her ears. "I know Chris will believe us and all, but it's just that I wish...oh, you know. I just wish we could have told him ourselves first."

I nodded. I was already wishing we didn't have to tell him at all.

Chris must have been watching for us. He came right over as we walked in the door.

"Hi, honey." He squeezed Ivy's shoulder and smiled at me. "Hello, Lizzie."

I smiled back. I began to feel a little better. He didn't look like he was angry. Maybe he didn't know about the notes. Maybe everything was going to be all right. But then he said, "Why don't we go into my office," and I knew it was serious after all.

Chris's office was behind the reference desk area. I'd never been in it before. It was really tiny and jammed with books. On top of his desk was an old picture of Ivy with short hair.

"Please sit down," he said.

I sat next to Ivy on the edge of one of the folding chairs. I could feel the cold of the metal right through my jeans.

Chris sat down behind his desk and cleared his throat. For a moment, no one said a word. I peeked at Ivy. She was chewing on the ends of her hair. That was a bad sign.

"Well." Chris cleared his throat again. My heart started to beat faster. He put the tips of his fingers together and stared at them. "It has been...er...brought to my attention that you girls have been spending an inordinate amount of time uptown lately, especially around the bank."

I didn't know what the word *inordinate* meant, but the rest was pretty clear. EvaLynne had tattled. I could feel my face getting hot. I hoped he wasn't going to yell at us.

"Now certain people don't want to complain," Chris said quickly. "They really don't, but they've found these notes very distracting. Of course I know that you didn't mean any harm and that it was just a big game but—"

"It's not a big game!" I said. "We were trying to save EvaLynne and the bank from the GPB!"

51

Then the whole story spilled out as Ivy and I interrupted each other trying to explain.

"We didn't really know that he was a crook," Ivy began. "Not at first anyway, even though he did have on those funny sunglasses. You know, the mirror kind? In fact, I sort of thought Lizzie was making it all up, but—"

"But the very next day we saw him again in the park," I said. "He was hiding behind the newspaper and watching the bank; and then EvaLynne came out, and he started following her!"

"EvaLynne?" Chris frowned.

"And then we saw him today," Ivy said. "Well, Lizzie saw him. This time he was hiding in a white truck with a little penguin on the side."

"He was just sitting there," I said. "Just..." I tried to think of a way to describe him. "...just like a great big red spider." I shivered, remembering.

"Just a minute, just a minute." Chris ran his fingers through his hair. "What is a GBB and what does a white penguin have to do with all this?"

"No, the penguin is on the truck," Ivy said.

"And the GPB is the Green Pillowcase Bandit," I finished for her. "Mr. Bennett told us—well, my parents—all about him. He's a bank robber."

"A bank robber?"

"Uh-huh, it's true," I said. "Really! Even the police know about him."

Chris sighed and tugged on his mustache. "Let's start over, okay? And go slower. I think I've missed something."

So Ivy and I slowed down and tried to explain it all over again, but somehow it still didn't come out right. I could tell that he didn't believe us. He had that same look on his face that Mom gets when she thinks Mitch or I am fibbing. Only Chris was more polite. He called it "jumping to conclusions."

"But, Chris, we really did see him hiding in the truck!" Ivy said. "And he was in the park. We saw him. Honest!"

52

"I'm sure you did," he said. "But that doesn't mean he's a...a *bank robber!*"

Just the way he said it made me squirm. He made it sound so dumb.

"I'm glad you told me," he went on. "Really I am, but I think you've let your imaginations run away with you. You know, Ivy, once you get to know her, I think you'll find that EvaLynne is a very nice person."

EvaLynne? We weren't really talking about her. At least not that way. But Chris was looking at Ivy, not me. Ivy chewed on her hair and didn't answer.

With a sigh, Chris stood up. "Well, I don't want to belabor the point. Let's just not have any more notes, okay?" His brown eyes crinkled up in the corners, but it was hard to smile back. "And promise me that you'll stay out of the bank unless, of course, you're expressly invited."

As we left the library, Ivy wouldn't look at me. I knew she was embarrassed because Chris hadn't believed us after all.

"Ivy?" I poked her. "Ivy, it's all right. At least we tried."

"He thinks we made up the story because I don't like her." Ivy's voice was so low, I almost missed some of the words. "He thinks I lied."

"No, he doesn't." I tried to make her feel better. "He just said we were jumping to conclusions. Mom says that to me all the time."

"That's not the same thing." Ivy kicked at a stone. It skipped across the sidewalk and disappeared into the grass. "And now what are we going to do?"

"I don't know." And I didn't. Mom and Dad love me and all. I know that. But would they believe me? I could just hear Mom now. "Lizzie is so dramatic. Every time she sees a fish, she calls it a whale." If Chris didn't believe us...I shook my head. "My folks would never believe us," I said.

"What about Mitch? I bet he would."

Would he? For a second I was tempted. Then I shook my head. "No, he'd just laugh and tell Peabrain, and then they'd both laugh."

"Maybe he wouldn't." When I didn't answer, she said, "Lizzie, you don't think we should tell the police, do you?"

The police! I thought of Chief of Police Travis with his big bull-froggy voice. He comes to our school every year to talk about traffic safety.

"I mean, if we were wrong . . ." Ivy looked worried.

I knew what she meant. If we were wrong, we'd be in a whole lot of trouble. Serious trouble.

I sighed. "I guess there's only one thing we can do."

"Give up?" Ivy's voice was hopeful.

"No, find more proof."

Ten

Bobbing Lights

"More proof. We need more proof." I was still talking about it the next day as Ivy and I walked over to Baby Imogene's house. "And the only place we're going to find it is at the bank because that's where he'll be." I pulled on my lip. "What we need is some kind of disguise. A really good one."

When Ivy didn't answer, I gave her a poke. "What's wrong? You haven't said two words since you came over."

Ivy made a face. "EvaLynne called last night."

"She did! Last night? What did she say?"

"She didn't call *me*. She called Chris."

"Well, what did she say to him?"

Ivy shook her head. "That's the trouble. I don't know. But whatever it was, it took her a long time to say it. It seemed like Chris was on the phone for hours."

"Oh, boy. Maybe she saw us last Saturday after all and decided to tell Chris about that, too."

"Probably." Her voice was glum. "She's just the kind of person who would tattle on you twice."

Mrs. Morely was waiting for us at the front gate. "I'm so

glad you're here. Imogene's waiting for you." She pointed toward the garden.

"Hello, Imogene," we called.

"Worrrrrm," she shouted. It looked like she was beating the tomato plants to death with her toy rake. "Worrrrrm."

"What did she say?" I asked.

"Worm. That's her newest word." Mrs. Morely shook her head. "Everything is a worm right now.'"

After she explained about Imogene's bottle and where the extra diapers were, Mrs. Morely pointed to the pile of blankets on the grass. "Try and have Imogene take a nap," she said. "Imogene can manage without one, but I don't think you girls can."

"What do you think she meant by that?" Ivy said as the car drove away. We found out almost immediately.

"Worrrrrm." Imogene came running up from the garden, waving a dirty fist at us. "Worrrrm."

"Oh, no, you don't think she's really found one, do you?"

When she came close enough, Ivy grabbed her by her little flowered skirt.

"Let me see, Imogene." She had to unpeel Imogene's fingers one by one.

"No, it's not a worm," Ivy told her. "It's a stick. Stick."

Imogene frowned. "Noooooo." She gave her hand a shake and pulled away. "Noooo." She started to run off again when Ivy called her.

"Hey, Imogene. I know where we can find a worm." She began digging in Imogene's wooden sandbox with one of the little plastic shovels. "Here, worm," she called.

Imogene came trotting back as if led by a string. "No, me," she said. She grabbed the shovel away from Ivy. "Here, worm, worm." Sand sprayed over the edge of the sandbox and onto the grass. "Here, worm."

After Imogene got tired of digging for worms, Ivy and I helped her make a worm castle. That was Ivy's idea. Then we made worm sand pies and worm cakes and worm cookies.

"Isn't this nice?" I said. But Imogene had other ideas.

"Booom!" she shouted. She pushed over the top of the castle. "Boom, boom!" She stomped on the pies.

Ivy and I looked at each other.

"I think it's time for a nap," I announced.

"Noooo!" Imogene shrieked. Then she really started to cry.

"Now I know why Mrs. Morely was so glad to see us," I muttered.

"Imogene?" Ivy looked around for something to distract her. "Hey, do you want to help us make a tent?"

Baby Imogene stopped mid-howl. We both looked at Ivy. A tent?

Ivy grabbed up two of the blankets off the ground and began to drape them over the clothesline. Then I caught on too. "Oh yes, a tent!"

We pinned the tops of the blankets together with clothes-pins and weighed down the bottoms with pails filled with sand. Imogene loved it.

"Now we can crawl inside," Ivy said. "But we have to be very good and quiet."

At first Imogene climbed all over us, but then she settled down between us and began to suck her thumb.

"I think she's going to take a n-a-p," Ivy said softly.

Sure enough. Imogene's eyes were beginning to close. Except for the sand in her hair, she looked as sweet as a picture book baby.

Ivy and I lay very still with our heads on our arms. The only sound was the soft flap-flapping of the blanket edges in the breeze. Baby Imogene began to make little purring sounds with her thumb still in her mouth.

I'd almost fallen asleep too, when I heard a screen door bang. It was Delight Nelson, next door. She was wearing her floppy white gardening hat and carrying a pair of shears. Right behind her came her cat.

"Gosh," Ivy whispered. "That's the biggest cat I've ever seen."

"*That* is Missy Megs. She's so mean I think even Basil is

afraid of her." The tip of the cat's white tail twitched as if she'd heard me.

"Oh, he wouldn't be scared of a cat." Ever since Ivy found out that Basil was really Mitch's dog, she was always sticking up for him. That reminded me of something. "Hey, have you seen Mitch's whistle? I can't find it any place."

Ivy got a funny look on her face. "Ah . . . er . . ."

"You-whooo!" Mrs. Nelson suddenly waved her shears in the air. "Mitchell!"

Mitch? I cautiously poked my head out of the tent and looked around. Mitch was walking down the alley toward home.

"Come and get some zinnias for your mother."

"Poor Mitch," Ivy whispered. "She'll talk his ear off."

"Oh, it's good for him." But I was glad she'd caught him and not me.

"Let me give you some of these pretty snapdragons too," Mrs. Nelson said. Her head popped down below the white picket fence to cut the flowers and then up again to talk to Mitch. Up and down. Up and down. She never seemed to run out of breath or flowers. She was telling him something about Missy Megs's pedigree. My eyes were beginning to close when suddenly I heard the words *bobbing lights*.

". . . two of them last Sunday night!" she was saying. "It was just after dark and I happened to look out of my kitchen window and there they were. Bobbing lights—flashlights—right in our alley, right where you're standing now! Then they took off up the alley."

"Really?" Mitch was practically hanging over the fence. "Did you see who they were?"

"No, but I can guess where they were headed—the Wentworth place!"

"The what?" Ivy asked but I poked her to be quiet. The Wentworth place! I didn't want to miss a word of this.

"Are you sure?" Mitch's voice cracked the way it always did when he was excited. "What makes you think that?"

That's exactly what I wanted to know.

"Where else could they be going?" Mrs. Nelson said.

"After the Morelys'—" She waved her shears in our direction. Ivy and I both ducked. "—and the Paynes' and Johansens', there aren't any more houses, just Williams Road and then fields and then the Wentworth place."

She stooped down to snip some more flowers. I thought I heard her say something about police.

"What?" I whispered to Ivy.

"What?" Mitch asked. "Excuse me?"

"I said—" Mrs. Nelson straightened up and handed Mitch a fistful of bachelor's buttons. "I said that the next time I see those lights, I'm going to call the police and report them. They're nothing but vandals, I'm sure of it. Just looking for trouble. You read about them in the newspaper every day. And they're all from Detroit, you know."

She stepped back and admired the huge bouquet Mitch was holding. "What do you think of those pretty posies, heh, Megs?" Then she tipped her head back to look at Mitch. "And Mitchell, don't go telling everyone about those lights. If they ever come back, I'll take care of them."

"I won't say a word," Mitch said. "Promise."

"But what about this Wentworth house?" Ivy whispered as soon as it was safe.

"Place," I said automatically. "Wentworth place. You mean, you were here all last summer and never heard of it?"

"Well, I've *heard* of it. Isn't it just some big old house that nobody lives in anymore?"

"Some big old house!" I couldn't believe it. She made it sound almost boring. "I guess you haven't heard enough about it then," I said, "because the Wentworth place is a whole lot more than that!"

Eleven

A Brush with
the Wentworth Ghost

"Well, then tell me." Ivy nudged me with her elbow. "Come on, tell me what's so special about it."

"Everything! But I bet Delight Nelson is wrong about those lights. About where they were going and all. Nobody in his right mind would go the Wentworth place after dark like that."

"Why not?"

"Because they just wouldn't," I said impatiently. "It's way out in the middle of the fields, and there's nobody around for miles—well, for a long ways—and there are all sorts of scary stories about that place. Some people think that it might even be haunted." I didn't want to admit that sometimes I was one of them.

"Haunted!" Ivy said. "Really?" At the sound of her voice, Baby Imogene sighed, and her thumb popped out of her mouth. For a long minute neither one of us dared to move.

"Really?" Ivy whispered again. Then she caught herself.

"Chris says that ghosts are just figments of people's imaginations."

"He does?" I thought a minute. "What's a figment, anyway?"

"A figment is a ..." She frowned. "I think he means ghosts aren't real; they don't exist."

"Don't exist! Doesn't he read the newspaper?" Then I told her all about the article in Sunday's paper. "Even *they* said the house is haunted." I didn't mention the fact that they said it was only haunted by sighs of its past. I wanted her on my side.

"And wait until you see it. It's this huge big house"—I spread out my arms to show her how big—"and it's surrounded by this great, big black iron fence that must be seven feet tall! And sometimes at night people driving by on the old Green Hills highway have seen tiny flickering lights in the attic or sometimes in the cellar."

"Really?" Ivy breathed.

I nodded. "But what's really scary are the bloodstains. Four of them. They lead right down to the cellar." I'd never seen them, but I'd heard all about them plenty of times. Ricky Terris, the boy who sat in front of me last year, said they were still bright red and sticky, but I wasn't so sure about that part. Then I had another thought. "Gosh, you don't think those could be *Mrs. Wentworth's* bloodstains, do you?"

"Sssshhh, not so loud," Ivy said but it was too late. Baby Imogene's eyelids fluttered. The next minute she was wide awake. And wet and hungry. It took two of us to change her diaper because once we got the wet one off, she escaped and ran around the yard squealing until we caught her again. Then she screeched for her bottle. By the time Mrs. Morely came home, it seemed more like two days had passed than two hours.

"There must be an easier way to make money," I said to Ivy as we walked back to my house.

"Maybe. But I bet it wouldn't be as much fun."

"Fun!" But then I giggled. "I'm just glad no one saw us

chasing Imogene around the yard trying to get her diaper back on. Who would have thought she could run that fast?"

When we got home, there was a note from Mom taped to the refrigerator door. She'd gone to the university library to do more research on her paper. "Have a snack," she wrote on the bottom of the note. "I'm sure you both deserve it."

"I think we deserve a medal." I opened the refrigerator and poked around for something to eat. "There's watermelon, plums, apples, or peanut butter sandwiches."

"Peanut butter," Ivy said just the way I knew she would. Peanut butter is the only kind of squishy food she'll eat.

Two seconds after Ivy and I had settled down on the back porch, Basil appeared. He always knows when there's food around.

"Oh, no, you don't." When I protected my sandwich with my elbow, he wiggled over to Ivy.

"You're nothing but a beggar," I told him. Basil wagged his tail but kept his eyes fixed on Ivy.

With a sigh, Ivy peeled off her crust for him. He caught it delicately before it hit the porch.

I stared across the backyard to the alley. "I wish I'd seen those bobbing lights. I'd love to know who was out there."

"Maybe they really were vandals from Detroit."

"I doubt it." I giggled. "Tell me, if you were a vandal, would you really drive all the way out *here?*"

From the kitchen behind us came the sudden sound of footsteps and low voices. It was Mitch and...darn, Peabrain was with him.

"Let's go," I whispered, but then I heard the word *Toro* and straightened up to listen.

"We'll have to be more careful," Mitch was saying.

Billy mumbled something I couldn't hear.

"Well, it would just be the end of everything if anybody found out," Mitch said. I heard the snap of the refrigerator door as it opened. "Boy, we'd be in so much trouble, we'd have to reach up to touch bottom."

I could barely sit still. Trouble? What kind of trouble?

If it hadn't been for greedy old Basil, we might have

found out, but he had heard the refrigerator door opening too. Before we could grab him, he was at the screen door, whining to be let in.

"Quick!" But it was too late to hide. Mitch was already at the back door. Billy Hunt came up behind him. "Well, if it isn't Lizzie Lizard, and this must be Poison Ivy."

"Ha, very funny!" I said and turned my back on them both. I'd hoped they'd go away, but just to spite us, they came out with their hunks of watermelon and sat above us on the porch railing.

"Just ignore them," I said loudly to Ivy. But that was hard to do, especially after Peabrain began spitting his watermelon seeds over our heads.

Ivy lasted about two seconds. Then she gave me a poke. I knew what she wanted, but I wasn't going to let them run us off. We were here first. Besides, maybe we could find out something. Not about that Toro person. I knew better than to ask about him, especially in front of Peabrain, but maybe we could find out what Mitch thought about those bobbing lights and where they were headed—or not headed.

I cleared my throat. "Mitch?" I knew I'd have to be tricky. "Do you think the Wentworth place is really haunted?"

There was total silence behind us. I guess I'd been too tricky. "I mean, do you think anybody would go there? After dark, I mean. I was telling Ivy—"

Billy interrupted me. "Lizard—I mean, Lizzie, if I were you, I'd stay away from that place. Far away."

"Wait—" Mitch began, but Billy went right on.

"That's no place for girls."

"For girls!" I jumped up and glared at him. "What do you mean 'for girls'?"

That took Peabrain by surprise. "I mean, that's not a good place for anybody to go any time."

That made me feel better. "Why not?"

"Well . . . I just remember what happened to me when I went there. Mitch knows all about it. He was there too."

"You were?"

Mitch looked uncomfortable. "He was?" I asked Billy.

"Remember the last day of school?" Billy said. "Remember how bright the moon was that night?"

I nodded, but I couldn't remember. That was weeks ago.

"Well, it started off as sort of a dare—a goof, really," Billy said. "We were talking about scary things, and I bet Mitch that he'd be too scared to go to the Wentworth place at night and he said he wasn't, so I said, 'I dare you,' and he said, 'I double dare you,' so then we both had to go. To win the bet we had to go all the way up to the front door and knock three times."

"You had to go after dark? At night?" I couldn't believe Mitch would be so dumb.

"It wasn't so bad at first," Billy said. "We walked up the alley and across the fields and then stopped at the black iron fence. Brother!" He shook his head. "When I saw that house I was ready to turn back, but then we flipped to see who had to go first, and I lost."

He paused for so long, I was afraid he wasn't going to tell us what happened next, but then he went on. "So I started up the front walk. Sort of stumbling, you know, because all the bricks in the sidewalk were loose." He moved his shoulders from side to side to show us how he had to walk over the loose bricks. "But then as I got a little closer, I thought I heard something. Something...I don't know... like moaning or something."

Ivy leaned a little closer. "Maybe it was the wind."

I could tell by her voice that she was hoping this was going to turn out to be one of those figments Chris had told her about, but I wasn't so sure.

"I thought it was the wind too," Billy said. "At least that's what I was hoping it was, but..." His eyes grew huge. "...but when I got almost up to the porch, I could see that the door was open."

"Open?" I whispered.

"Open," Billy repeated. "Just as if someone—or something—knew we were coming. Then all of a sudden the door began to swing. Squeeeeeeak. Squeeeeeeak.

"And that's when I heard something moving inside, something slow and heavy. And the door began to swing faster and faster. Squeeeeeeeak, squeeeeeeeak!"

"Then what happened?" I couldn't stand it anymore.

"Then I took off and ran like the devil," Billy said. He sagged against the porch railing. "And I've never been back since."

For a second, Ivy and I just stared at him. "But...but..." I started to sputter. "...but how could a door just swing like that? You must have seen *something*. Come on, tell us!"

Billy shrugged. "There isn't anything left to tell. I can't explain what happened. I don't know if anyone can."

"But Mitch, didn't you see anything?" I asked. "Didn't you hear anything?"

"He was too far away," Billy said. "He was still at the iron fence. But I can tell you one thing. We were lucky to get away at all."

"But..." I wasn't ready to give up yet. "...but how could you see that the door was open if it was dark out?"

"Moonlight," Billy said promptly.

I opened my mouth and closed it again. I couldn't believe it. Billy Hunt and my very own brother had had a brush with the Wentworth ghost.

Twelve

Too Many Mysteries

A ghost. A real ghost. Well, probably a ghost. I kept eyeing
Mitch all through dinner that night. How could he just sit
there eating chicken and cole slaw when he had seen—
maybe almost seen—the Wentworth ghost? How could anybody be the same after something like that?

In fact, there were a whole bunch of things I still didn't
understand. Like why didn't he and Billy go right back to
the Wentworth place the very next morning and do some
investigating? That's what *I* would have done. Well, Ivy and
I. What if it really had been a ghost? If I'd come that close
to one, I'd want to know it. I know what Billy said, but
still...didn't Mitch see *anything*? Anything at all? I
couldn't wait to get him alone and find out some answers.

But getting Mitch alone and in one place was harder to
do than I thought.

"Mitch?" I trailed after him as he did about fifty million
little fix-it jobs that he was supposed to have done months
ago.

"Mitch, I want to ask you something."

"Ask me later."

"It will just take a minute."

"Later! Can't you see I'm busy?"

"Okay, but you don't have to get mad. Just come get me when you're done, promise? It's important."

Restless, I wandered through the dining room. Mom was hunched over the portable typewriter, staring at a blank sheet of paper in the roller.

"Mom?"

"What?" Her voice was grim.

"Ah..." I was going to ask her what she thought about ghosts, but I could tell this wasn't exactly the best time. "What's your paper about?" I asked instead.

"Humor," she snapped.

"Oh." I tiptoed around her and into the living room where Dad was reading the newspaper. I perched on the arm of his chair reading over his shoulder until he shook the pages at me.

I slid to my feet. "Dad?"

"Hmmmm?"

"Do you believe in ghosts? I mean, do you think they might, just might be real?"

"Honey, you know better than that." He didn't even lift his eyes from the paper. "Ghosts are just figments of people's imaginations."

I sighed. Sometimes I think all parents are alike.

Then I heard the back door bang softly and footsteps in the kitchen. Mitch must have finished whatever he had been doing to the lawn mower. I waited, but he didn't come into the living room. The back stairs creaked.

"'Night, Dad," I said quickly and scooted up the stairs after him. I'd almost caught up with him when he ducked into the bathroom and closed the door.

"Mitch?"

"For heaven's sake, I'm in the *bathroom!*"

"Sorry." I backed up and waited in the middle of the hall-way—and waited and waited. There wasn't a sound from the other side of the door. Suddenly I realized that he wasn't planning on coming out, at least not while I was there. That made me mad. If he thought he could outwait me, he had another thought coming.

I clumped down the hall, opened my bedroom door and closed it again with a loud snap. Then I sneaked across the hall and slipped into Mitch's room. I closed the door softly behind me. So there, Mitchell Bruce!

Now that I was in Mitch's room, I thought of something else. Keeping my hands behind my back so Mitch couldn't accuse me of snooping, I snooped around for that big rectangular "something" that he and Peabrain had carried out of Jake's Pet Shop. It wasn't on the floor or on top of the bookcase. I peeked into his closet. Nope, it wasn't there either. On Mitch's desk was an open book. I sidled over to see what it was and then wished I hadn't.

"Ugh!"

It was a picture of a poor little mouse being squeezed to death by a huge snake. Beneath the picture it said:

Some snakes are constrictors. They do not kill their prey with poison as the pit vipers do. Instead, they seize their prey with their mouths and then loop themselves around it. The victims are not squeezed to death as popularly thought, but are suffocated. Every time the victim exhales, the snake tightens its grip until the victim dies of lack of oxygen.

I shivered. Good grief. How could Mitch read stuff like that? I closed my eyes, but I could still see that poor little mouse.

Suddenly the door opened behind me. I spun around and stood face-to-face with Mitch.

"All right, Lizard, what are you doing in here?" he demanded.

"I didn't touch anything, honest," I said quickly. "I was waiting for you. There's something important I want to ask you."

Mitch folded his arms across his chest. I knew I was going to have to talk fast.

"I've been thinking about what Billy said. You know, about the Wentworth place? Well, *something* must have made that door swing. Are you sure you didn't see anything that night? Maybe something moving in the moonlight?"

"I don't want to talk about it."

"Huh?"

"I said, I don't want to talk about it."

"But what if it was a ghost? Maybe Ivy and I could help you solve—"

"No." He put his hands on my shoulders, turned me around and pushed. Two seconds later I was standing back out in the hallway on the other side of the closed door.

"Okay, Mitch, you'll be sorry," I yelled. "Ivy and I are going to solve this all by ourselves, and when we do, we're not going to tell you a thing about it. Nothing!"

Silence. I marched across to my own room and slammed my door behind me. Kicking off my shoes, I flopped down on the bed. I couldn't believe it, but suddenly there were just too many mysteries. Too many mysteries, and I hadn't solved one of them yet.

I counted on my fingers. One—the really big one—the mysterious stranger. Was he *really* the Green Pillowcase Bandit? I was sure, almost sure he was, but what good did that do if nobody else believed us? We still had to find more proof, proof that even the police would believe.

And then there was Mitch. I frowned and pulled on my lip. Mom was right. There was something funny going on. No, I take that back. There were lots of funny things going on. Sam Toro for one. Who was this guy? And then there was all that talk about something being too expensive and too risky; and Mitch being broke when he should be rolling in money and last Sunday night's disappearance. And now the Wentworth ghost. And Mitch didn't want to talk about it!

I groaned and stared up at the ceiling. I wished Ivy were here.

A car swung up the street; its headlights flashed through my window. That reminded me of Mrs. Nelson's bobbing lights. I'd forgotten about them for a second. There was another mystery. Why would anyone go walking down our alley at night with flashlights? Hmmm, maybe they were just walking their dog, I told myself. But at night? I shook my head. Probably not. Besides, Basil would have barked if there had been a dog out there. Maybe they were just goofing around, but somehow I doubted it. What if Mrs. Nelson was right? What if they were headed toward the Wentworth place? I sat up. What if they went there every night after dark? There was only one way to find out.

I peeked out my door. Mitch's light was still on, and I could hear him moving around. I'd have to be careful. I didn't want any surprises. I tiptoed down the hall and into the tiny guest bedroom. I didn't dare turn on a light. I felt my way across the rug and onto the cool tile floor of the even tinier bathroom. Stepping into the tub, I pulled up on the window. It slid up without a sound. Perfect. I could see all the way to the edge of Baby Imogene's garden.

It was much darker in the house than out. There was still some blue left in the sky. I took a deep breath. I could smell Mrs. Nelson's roses and, from somewhere down the block, freshly mowed grass. Leaning my elbows on the windowsill, I watched and waited—and waited. The maple trees slowly turned black against the sky. Soon it would be really dark.

I yawned, rubbing one cold foot against the other. I wished something would happen. From two doors down I could hear Baby Imogene wailing. They must be trying to put her to bed. When Imogene was really little, she'd only fall asleep in the car. It seemed as if every night last summer we'd see Mr. Morely carrying her out to the car and then driving around the block until Imogene finally fell asleep. They didn't have to do that anymore, but Imogene still hated to go to bed.

I yawned again. Maybe I should give up and go to bed too. It seemed silly to wait any longer. Suddenly I blinked.

There! There in Mrs. Nelson's backyard, near the clump of daylilies, a shadow moved. I pushed my head against the screen trying to see what it was. It moved again. It was Delight Nelson! But what was she doing out there?

I stared at her, waiting, but now she was as still as a statue. She reminded me of Missy Megs. I'd seen Megs freeze like that when she was hunting. Hunting! That's exactly what Mrs. Nelson was doing. She was hiding out in her garden, waiting and watching for the bobbing lights!

Thirteen

Kidnapped?

Just before the phone rang the next day, Ivy and I were playing Monopoly at the dining room table. It was the coolest spot we could find in the house.

Ivy was counting her paper money under the table so that I wouldn't be able to see if she had enough to buy Park Place or not. "Then what happened?" she asked.

"Nothing. That's the problem." I was telling her about last night. "I waited and waited but nothing happened. Finally Mrs. Nelson went inside, so I went to bed too. It sure gave me a creepy feeling, though, watching her." I shook my head, remembering. "And do you want to hear something else funny? Do you know what Mitch said when I asked him about that night at the Wentworth place? 'I don't want to talk about it.' Can you believe it? He sounded like some kind of movie star!"

"Maybe he doesn't want to talk about it." Ivy plunked down a fistful of money. "Here. This is for Park Place, and the bank owes me two hundred dollars."

As I handed her the money, I said, "Well, if it had been

me who had seen that door swinging and heard that moaning, I'd want to know what it was all about." I watched Ivy's lips move as she recounted the money. She added it to the hidden pile in her lap. "In fact, I still do," I hinted. "Don't you?"

"Uh-uh." She shook her head. "Not me. I've done enough investigating for one day."

"But we didn't find anything," I pointed out. Ivy and I had spent the morning uptown. We didn't dare go into the bank. Instead we spent the whole time across the street on a park bench, hiding behind yesterday's newspaper. But we didn't see a trace of the mysterious stranger or his truck. Deep down inside, I was sort of glad. Maybe he'd given up on our bank and left town.

"Aren't you even curious about the Wentworth place?" I asked. "Don't you even want to see it?"

That's when the phone rang.

"Here, you can shake the dice for me." I started for the kitchen, but Mom got there first.

"Hello?" Then her voice changed. "What? Who's missing?"

"Missing!"

Mom gestured me to be quiet. Ivy crept into the kitchen to listen too.

"Yes, Delight," Mom said. "But no, I haven't seen her."

Her? Ivy and I looked at each other. I knew we were both thinking the same thing: EvaLynne Hayes! She'd been kidnapped right from under our noses. But how did Mrs. Nelson know?

"Just a minute," Mom said. "They're right here. I'll ask them." She turned to us. "Delight Nelson says Missy Megs is missing. Have you seen her?"

"Missy Megs? The cat?"

"Of course." Mom gave me one of her eagle-eye looks. "Who do you think I meant?"

"Nobody. I mean, no, we haven't seen her."

There was a sudden squawk from the phone. Mom pulled

73

the receiver back to her ear. "No, they haven't seen her, Delight. Yes, of course, we'll keep an eye out for her."

Two seconds after Mom hung up the phone, there was a rap on the back screen door. It was Mrs. Nelson. She had on a ruffled pink housecoat and slippers.

"I was just getting ready for my nap," she began as if she were in the middle of a conversation instead of just starting one. "And I took Missy Megs out to the backyard and tied her up just the way I do every afternoon," she said. "You know."

We nodded. Everyone in the whole neighborhood knew her schedule. It never varied all summer long.

"Well," she continued, "I got into bed, but I couldn't sleep. It was too hot. So after about twenty minutes I got up and went outside to untie Megs, but she was gone! Kidnapped! Stolen right out of my own backyard."

Behind her glasses, Mrs. Nelson's blue eyes filled with tears. I felt really sorry for her. I could tell Mom did too.

"Don't worry, it will be all right." Mom patted her hand. "I'm sure the cat just wandered off."

"No, she was kidnapped," Mrs. Nelson insisted. "She couldn't have broken loose on her own. Come on, I'll show you the rope."

We all trooped next door, and Mrs. Nelson held up the piece of clothesline that she had tied to Megs's collar. The other end was still tied to the tree. "See, it's a good, strong rope, and there's not a tooth mark on it. Someone had to untie it."

"But who would want to steal your cat?" Mom said gently.

Mrs. Nelson straightened up her shoulders. "Anyone might. Missy Megs is an extraordinary cat."

The way she said it almost gave me goose bumps. "Ivy and I can help you look," I offered. "What do you want us to do?"

"Oh, if you'd look along the alley, I'll check the street!" She started for the front gate and then swerved toward the house. "No, I'd better finish calling all the neighbors first.

Maybe they've seen her. Where's Mitchell? Maybe he can help too."

"He's over at Billy's," Mom said. "But I'll tell him when he gets home."

Ivy and I walked first up the alley and then down, peering under all the shrubs and bushes. "Here kitty, kitty," we called. "Here, kitty."

"Worrrrrrm!" answered Imogene from her own backyard. She was busy in the sandbox. It looked as if she were burying her blanket. Mrs. Morely gave us a tired wave from under the faded black umbrella she was using for shade.

"Have you seen Mrs. Nelson's big white cat?" I called.

Mrs. Morely shook her head. "Delight called and asked me that already. This is the first time we've been out all day."

When we got to the Johansens' big elm, we stopped for a minute in the shade. "Here, kitty. Here, Megs." From the street, we could hear Mrs. Nelson calling for her now too.

"Isn't it funny such a big cat could just disappear?" Ivy said. "I wonder if she's stuck up in a tree somewhere." She tipped her head back and peered up into the branches of the old elm.

"She's too smart for that." But I stopped fanning myself with my hand and looked up too. There was a beautiful black and yellow butterfly fluttering around the leaves. It rested for a minute on a branch and then sailed across the road to the Indian Trail.

The Indian Trail wasn't really a trail, and it didn't belong to the Indians, but that's what we've always called it. Maybe it was farmland a long time ago, but now it was just huge rolling fields of brambles and wild flowers. Beyond the fields was the old Green Hills highway. And in between...

"Hey, Ivy?"

"What? Do you see her?"

"No, but look." I pointed out the line of poplars at the edge of the fields. "Guess what's just on the other side of those trees? The Wentworth place!"

I didn't even get a chance to finish before Ivy was shaking her head. "Oh no, Lizzie. We promised Mrs. Nelson that we were going to look for her cat, not chase ghosts, remember?"

"Well, there's no reason why we can't do both. Mrs. Nelson's always bragging about what a great hunter Megs is. Maybe she's off chasing field mice. Or moles. Come on, don't you want to just see the place?" I knew I'd never go by myself; Ivy had to come. "All we'll do is look. *Please?*"

Ivy hesitated, fiddling with a long piece of string around her neck. I'd never noticed it before. Attached to it was a lumpy "something" hidden by her blouse. When she saw me looking at the string she dropped her hand. "Oh, all right. But you're the one who told me that *no one* ever goes to the place."

"Well, not at night. But wait until you see it," I said. "You won't be sorry."

It was even hotter out in the fields. We followed the old bike path through clumps of field daisies and Queen Anne's lace. I realized that I had just been kidding myself when I said we could look for the cat out here. There was no way we'd ever spot her. The weeds on either side of the path were almost waist high.

"We should have worn jeans," Ivy said. "And bug spray." She batted at the mosquitoes around her face. "I don't know why anybody would want to build his house way out here anyway."

"Taxes," I said. "At least that's what some people say. Mr. Wentworth didn't want to pay taxes, so he built his house just on the other side of the city limits. But *I* heard that he didn't want any nosy neighbors around." I didn't have to tell her which story I believed. "Of course, he didn't have to walk through these fields every time he went to town. The Green Hills highway goes practically right by his door."

"Hey." Ivy grabbed my arm. "There's Mitch and Billy." She pointed toward the trees. "Or at least there are two boys out there."

"Mitch is over at Peabrain's," I said, but I looked too.

A boy bounced up from the tall grass. It was Mitch all right. He had on the blue and gold Michigan T-shirt Mom gave him. A second later, I saw Billy.

"Quick, yell," Ivy said. "They can help us look for Megs."

"Wait, let's see what they're doing first."

It was easy to follow them. They were walking very slowly with their heads down as if they were looking for something. Then they'd stop. Just stop and stand there for what seemed like forever, and then they'd start walking again.

"What do you think they're doing?" Ivy asked.

"I don't know. I can't figure it out."

Mitch and Peabrain stopped again. Ivy and I crouched down and watched. Mitch bent down into the tall grass and picked something up. Something white and furry.

"Look," Ivy said. "It's Missy Megs!"

Fourteen

All Alone

"What on earth are they doing with Mrs. Nelson's cat?" I straightened up to take a better look. That was definitely Missy Megs. She looked mean even from here.

"They must have just found her," Ivy said. "Gosh, isn't that lucky? Mrs. Nelson is going to be so happy to see her."

"She sure will," I said slowly, "but I wonder what they're doing out here? They're supposed to be over at Billy's."

Ivy shrugged. "Well, it's a good thing they came along. Who knows if Megs could have found her way back home again." She brushed her hair off her face. "Now can't we go back? I'm frying. Maybe your mom will let us run under the sprinkler or something."

I didn't answer. I hated to give up now that we were so close to the Wentworth place. Then I noticed the boys were still walking toward the trees, Mitch holding Megs in his arms.

Ivy shaded her eyes with her hand. "Where do you think they're going now?"

I didn't know for sure, but I could guess. "Come on, let's follow them and see."

We trailed behind them, keeping our distance, but it was clear that they weren't worried about being followed. They were so busy talking that they never once looked back. And I was right about where they were going. We were headed straight for the Wentworth place.

When we reached the trees, we had to leave the path and wade through the weeds and pricker bushes. Huge pale green grasshoppers flew up from under our feet. Ivy squeaked every time one whizzed by, but then the house with its black iron fence came into full view. "Oh!" She stopped. "It's huge."

I nodded proudly. It was huge with its tall peaked roof and its great round tower over the porch, but even from here I could see that the white paint was peeling and the porch was beginning to sag. Remembering how beautiful it looked in that old picture in the *Tribune,* I wished I could have seen it when it was new.

"You've been here before?" Ivy asked.

"Just with Mitch." I didn't add that it had been a long time ago.

"It doesn't have any eyes," she said softly.

"Eyes!"

"Uh-huh, the windows. They're all boarded up. It looks like it's blind."

I wished she hadn't said that. It made the house seem almost alive. I thought of Billy walking up the broken brick path to the front door. Had something—someone—been watching him that night from behind one of those windows? Even in moonlight, even in a spotlight, you wouldn't catch me going up there. Then I had another thought. What if we were being watched right now? This very minute!

"Lizzie?"

I jumped. "What?"

Ivy was turning around in a slow circle. "Where's Mitch?"

"Mitch? Oh, boy." Somehow we'd lost them.

We ducked down and cautiously circled around to the back, making a wide loop. Every few feet we popped up over the weeds like a periscope, but we didn't spot the boys.

The back of the house was almost as fancy as the front, with another big porch and a wide brick path leading up to it. On either side of the walk there must have been gardens once, but now only wild roses were left mixed in with the weeds.

I took a step toward the path. "Oh, don't." Ivy grabbed my arm. "Don't go any closer."

"I thought you said ghosts were just figments of people's imaginations?" But I wouldn't have gone any closer anyway.

"That's what Chris said." She was still whispering. "Gosh, it feels like we're in the middle of nowhere."

"I know, but the highway to Green Hills is just on the other side of that hedge over there."

Ivy barely glanced toward the hedge. Something else had caught her eye. "Look, there they are."

I whirled around. The boys were past the trees already. Megs was a white, fluffy ball riding on Mitch's shoulder. "Shoot, they must have slipped right past us. I'll bet they're headed for home."

"Ssssh, listen," Ivy hissed. She pulled me down in the weeds.

I held my breath. Had she heard moaning? A door opening? Was Billy's what-ever-it-was going to come out and grab us?

For half a second all I could hear was the thudding of my heart. Then I heard it too. The heavy crunch of gravel. Someone had turned off the highway and was driving up the old road toward the house.

Then I heard the engine stop and the snap of the car door opening. All I could see over the hedge was the top of a white car. No, it couldn't be a car. It was too tall. It had to be a truck—a white truck.

My heart stopped. "Ivy, run!" I tugged on her arm, but

she had seen it too. She froze like a rabbit in the grass, too scared to move. "Ivy!"

But then it was too late. If we ran, he'd see us. I ducked down until my nose touched my knees, the weeds rustling over my head. I could hear his footsteps, crunching of the gravel beneath his feet. Then *thunk*. I flinched. He was on the brick path, walking toward us.

I tried to shrink into a ball, praying the weeds would cover us. Beside me, Ivy vibrated like a leaf.

The footsteps came closer and closer. I squeezed my eyes shut. Silence. Then a soft swishing sound. He was moving through the weeds. Don't stop, I prayed. Don't stop.

The footsteps stopped. I could feel him standing in front of us. I forced myself to lift my head. He was so close, I could see myself reflected in his black mirror sunglasses.

"Well, who do we have here? Two little girls all alone."

Then he smiled, and I'd never seen a man with such little teeth.

Fifteen

Basil's Discovery

For an awful second I couldn't move, couldn't breathe.

"Ah...we were...ah..." Slowly I straightened up, pulling Ivy up with me. "Ah..."

"We were looking for our cat," Ivy said. Her voice shook but she looked right at him. "Have you seen her?"

"Yes, our cat," I babbled. "She's a big, white one. Really big. And white too."

"I haven't seen any cat." He wasn't smiling anymore. "I've only seen you."

"Oh." My throat closed up.

"We have to go now," Ivy said loudly. Her fingers were icy on my arm. "My dad is waiting for us."

We turned and walked away as if in slow motion. Left foot, right foot, left foot, right foot. Through the weeds. Past the wide back porch. Past the boarded-up windows. Left foot, right foot, left——There was a soft sound behind us. We ran. Out through the black iron gates and into the fields. I couldn't find the path. Pricker bushes tore at our legs and snagged our clothes as we stumbled over the hidden ruts and hollows of the field.

"There's the road," I yelled. "Straight ahead."

Only after we had crossed Williams Road did we dare stop and glance over our shoulders. The field behind us was empty and silent under the baking sun.

I sagged against the Johansens' big elm, trying to catch my breath. "No, don't stop now," Ivy said. "We have to get home."

Together we limped down the alley and into my yard. "Mom?"

Basil was stretched out on the Welcome mat on the back porch. We had to step over him to open the door.

"Mom?" The house was still. I looked at the clock. It was only four-thirty. It seemed as if we'd been gone for hours and hours. "Mom?" Then I remembered. "She's in class. She won't be home until six."

"You mean there's nobody home?" Ivy whispered.

We both turned and looked toward the alley. Then without a word, we stepped inside and I latched the screen door.

"No, wait." Ivy opened the screen door again and coaxed Basil inside. Then she latched it, pushed the heavy wood door closed after it and locked that too.

My legs felt suddenly wobbly. I sat down on the kitchen floor, hugging Basil for comfort. We're okay, I told myself. We're okay. Everything's all right.

Ivy sat down beside me. I could feel her shivering even though it must have been ninety degrees in the kitchen now with all the doors closed. "Lizzie? As soon as your mom comes home, we're going to have to tell her. I mean"—her voice started to shake—"something horrible could have happened out there."

I nodded, hugging Basil closer. Something horrible could have happened. If it hadn't been for Ivy's quick thinking about her dad . . . I thought of that awful smile and shivered.

"But Ivy, what was he doing out there? The Wentworth

83

place is miles from the bank and EvaLynne. It's miles from anywhere."

"Maybe that's it," Ivy said slowly. "Maybe he thought no one would ever find him there. You said yourself that nobody ever goes near there."

"You mean the Wentworth place could be his hideout?" I hadn't thought of that. And Ivy was right. It would be perfect. No neighbors. Nobody around—"Hey, but what about Mitch and Peabrain? What do you think they were doing out there?"

Ivy looked worried. "I've been thinking about that too and—"

Suddenly there was a knock on the door. Basil gave a startled bark and scrambled to his feet. Ivy and I froze.

"You-whooo! Oh, you-whooo!"

There was no mistaking that voice. Delight Nelson. When I opened the door, she beamed at me through the screen.

"Megs is back! I just found her a few minutes ago."

"I know, Mitch—"

"Mitchell?" Mrs. Nelson looked puzzled. "I haven't seen him. I found Megs myself. She was hiding under my peony bushes. She must have gotten loose somehow, after all. Well, I just wanted to let you know." With a wave, she started down the porch steps. "And don't forget to tell your mother. I'm sure she'll want to know too."

I nodded automatically. "I will." But as I closed the door, I thought it was funny that Mitch had just dropped Megs off without telling Mrs. Nelson that he and Billy had found her way up on the Indian Trail.

Then I looked at the clock and forgot all about Megs. "Ivy, it's five o'clock. Mom will be home in an hour."

Suddenly I was nervous. Nervous and a little scared. I knew Mom was going to be really upset when we told her about the mysterious stranger, and I knew she'd tell Dad, and then Dad would call the police, and then the police— what would the police do? Arrest him? But he hadn't done anything really wrong. At least not yet. What really scared me was what if we were wrong about him? Then what? I wiped my sweaty hands on the back of my shorts.

"Ivy, maybe we'd better go through the clue book before we talk to Mom. Maybe we missed something."

I ran upstairs and brought it back down to the kitchen. Ivy restlessly circled the table as I flipped through the pages. "No, start at the beginning," she said. "The very beginning."

I turned back to page one. "'Bank.'" I read out loud. "'June 20th. Tall man with red hair. Mirror sunglasses. Briefcase with snaps. Acted nervous. Seen lurking by copy machine. Who is he?'"

"I wish we'd never seen him," Ivy said fiercely.

When I got to the part about sneaking down the alley behind EvaLynne's house and spotting Mr. Bennett, she interrupted me with a sniff. "We don't have to bother about that. That doesn't have anything to do with anything."

As it turned out, Ivy was wrong, but we didn't know it then.

On the top of the next page. I'd written two words: *Sam Toro*—and a question mark.

"You know," I said, "isn't it funny that Mitch and Peabrain keep whispering about this Sam Toro but we've never even seen him? Isn't that weird? If he's such a great friend, how come he never comes over? Look at Peabrain. He's always hanging around here."

Ivy stopped pacing and chewed on a strand of hair. "Maybe he's shy," she said. "Or..." She didn't finish.

"Or maybe Mitch doesn't want us to see him! Maybe he thinks Mom and Dad wouldn't like him." I pushed back my chair. "I'll bet we can at least find out where he lives." I ran and got the phone book.

"Hmmmm." I ran my finger down the list of T's. "Thomas, Thompson, Thompson—there must be a million Thompsons—Thorkel, Thorndike, Torvend, and Twight. Shoot, he's not here."

"'Toro' means bull," Ivy offered. "I learned that in Spanish class. Maybe his real name is Sam Bull and Toro is just a nickname."

I tried that too, but there weren't any Bulls listed in the phone book either.

"Maybe his family just moved here," Ivy said. "Or maybe he has a stepfather, and it's under the stepfather's name. Or maybe..."

"Or maybe Mitch has it upstairs in his room."

"Lizzie!" Ivy sounded shocked. "How would you like it if Mitch went snooping around in your room?"

"I'd kill him," I said. "But this is different. This could be important."

I had to practically drag Ivy up the stairs. "We're not going to hurt anything," I said. "We're just going to look."

Mitch's door was closed. I opened it very slowly just in case he had booby-trapped it—he did that once last summer—but this time nothing fell on me. Ivy tiptoed in behind me, her hands behind her back. Basil wasn't shy. He barged past us to sniff Clara, the guinea pig, through the bars of her cage.

"Be nice to Clara," I told him. I poked through the clutter on top of Mitch's desk and then peeked into his drawer. "I don't know how he finds anything in this mess."

"Lizzie, did you know that snakes don't have any eyelids?"

I looked up. Ivy was leafing through one of Mitch's library books.

"It says here that snakes have transparent lenses, a kind of scale, over each eye instead of eyelids. Isn't that something. Just think, they can sleep with their eyes open."

"Iveeeee, come on! You're supposed to be helping me." I turned around and caught Basil with his head in Mitch's closet.

"And you come out of there, Basil. There's nothing in there for you."

Basil's tail wagged against my leg, but he wouldn't budge.

"Come on, boy." I pushed his head away and peeked inside. "Gosh, if Mom saw this, she'd have a fit."

The floor of the closet was a jumble of shoes, dirty socks, pajamas and something else. I pulled it out into the light. It was a pillowcase. A green pillowcase. "Ivy, look!"

"What—oh!"

I could tell by her face what she was thinking: The Green Pillowcase Bandit.

"It must be your mother's," she said quickly, but I was already shaking my head. It wasn't my mother's. I knew that for sure because she has a thing about colored sheets and pillowcases. She thinks they're tacky. Everything of ours is white—boring white.

"Then it must be Billy's," she said.

When I didn't answer, she said, "You don't think . . . you don't really think—"

Downstairs a door banged and Mom's voice called out, "Lizzie? Mitch? I'm home."

Sixteen

Waiting for Mitch

"Quick, don't let your mom see that." Ivy snatched the pillowcase out of my hand and stuffed it back into the closet. She closed the closet door with a snap.

"But where'd it come from?" I whispered. "Ivy, what if that's *the* green pillowcase?" Mitch and the Green Pillowcase Bandit? My brother and a bank robber? I felt dizzy.

"Hello?" Mom called. "Anybody home?"

"Ah...coming." I lowered my voice to a whisper again. "Ivy, now what are we going to tell Mom about the mysterious stranger?"

"What do you mean? We have to tell her! You even said—"

"But don't you see? If he really is the Green Pillowcase Bandit, then Mitch could have gotten that pillowcase from him!"

"Oh, gosh. You mean, maybe he and Mitch...Oh, Lizzie, then we can't tell your mom anything. Not yet. Not until we've talked to Mitch. But it couldn't be true. I mean, lots of people have green pillowcases—"

"In their closets?"

She ignored me. "And it doesn't prove a thing. All we have to do is wait until Mitch comes home, and then he'll..." She seemed to run out of words. "Then he'll be able to explain everything," she finished.

"Lizzie, honey?"

There wasn't time to argue. I didn't want Mom coming up the stairs and finding us in Mitch's room. We shooed Basil out the door and started down the stairs after him.

"There you are." Mom smiled at us. "It sure is hot in here. How come everything was all closed up? I had to use my front door key to get in." Mom didn't wait for an answer. "I handed in my paper this afternoon." She opened the refrigerator and started pulling things out for dinner. "'The Element of Humor in *Pride and Prejudice*.' I thought I'd never get it done, but I did!" She put last night's roast on the counter and reached for the lettuce. "Wait until you girls read Jane Austen. You're going to love her. Her books are delicious."

Delicious? Delicious *books?*

Ivy nudged me. "Lizzie, Chris will be wondering where I am. He gets really worried if I'm late."

"But you can't leave now," I whispered. "You have to wait until Mitch comes home."

Mom saw us whispering. "It's all right. Ivy can stay for dinner. Don't be shy, honey. You know we love having you."

"You have to stay," I told her. "For Mitch's sake."

That did it. While Ivy called her father, Mom handed me the plates for the table, then the water glasses. It took me a second to realize that she'd only given me four.

"Isn't Dad coming home for dinner tonight?"

"He'll be here any second. Why?"

I counted out loud. "You and Dad and Ivy and me and Mitch. That's five."

Mom handed me the butter plate. "Oh, Mitch won't be here. He's having supper at Billy Hunt's tonight."

I swung around. "He is?" I looked at Ivy.

89

"Uh-huh. He asked me about it this morning. Heavens, those two are as thick as thieves lately."

Thieves. I flinched, thinking of the green pillowcase hidden upstairs. Could Mitch really be friends with a bank thief? No, not Mitch. He'd never get mixed up with somebody like that. But then I remembered what he had said yesterday to Peabrain in the kitchen: "... if anybody found out, we'd be in so much trouble, we'd have to reach up to touch bottom." I groaned. Oh, Mitch.

Dinner seemed to go on forever. I couldn't eat—not even the cold roast beef with Mom's horseradish sauce. Instead, I watched the clock. 6:56 ... 7:00 ... 7:03. If Mitch wasn't home by 7:30, I decided, then I was going to tell Mom and Dad everything—all about the mysterious stranger, the Wentworth place, the green pillowcase upstairs, Mitch—everything. But what if I was wrong about Mitch? Maybe the pillowcase belonged to Billy's mom. Or maybe they found it. But then why was it stuffed away in Mitch's closet? At 7:25, I decided that I'd wait until 8:00, but that was my absolute limit.

"You're awfully quiet tonight, Lizzie," Dad said. "I think the cat's got your tongue." He smiled at Ivy. "I think he's got both your tongues." Then he said something to Mom about Mr. Bennett.

"Mr. Bennett? Did he find out something about the bank robber?" I crossed my fingers. Maybe the police knew all about the mysterious stranger already. Maybe we wouldn't have to say anything after all.

"No, I think Wendell has other things on his mind right now."

"He does?" What could be more important than catching the Green Pillowcase Bandit? Then I remembered our notes. Had EvaLynne tattled to him too? Ivy looked like she wanted to slide under the table and disappear.

"In fact"—Dad looked over the top of his glasses at Mom—"I think that's why we've been invited over there tonight. He said he had something he wanted to tell us."

"Tonight? You're going over there tonight?"

"We won't be gone long," Mom said. "Just for dessert." When she saw the look on my face, she added, "Don't worry. I have dessert in the refrigerator for you two."

Dessert! As if I cared about dessert at a time like this. I looked at the clock. 7:32. Where was Mitch? What if he didn't get home before they left? Time had been dragging by, minute by minute, but now suddenly there wasn't any time left.

Dad finished his coffee and patted his pockets for the car keys. "Lock the door behind us, girls."

Mom handed me a sheet of paper. "Here's Mr. Bennett's phone number in case you need it. Now don't fight with Mitch while we're gone. There's enough dessert for all of you." She stopped at the door, still ticking things off on her fingers. "Don't let anyone in the house. Make sure you put the meat away and leave the kitchen neat. And you know, if you're bored, you and Ivy are welcome to try my Jane Austen."

"We won't—" The screen door slapped shut behind her. "—get bored," I finished.

For a long moment after we heard the car drive off, Ivy and I didn't say anything. Then Ivy went over to the table and began clearing away the dishes.

"What are you doing?"

"I'm going to do the dishes," she said. "And by the time we're finished, Mitch will be home, and he'll tell us all about the pillowcase."

"Do you really think so?"

Ivy nodded.

With a sigh, I started to help her clear, careful not to step on Basil as he trotted behind us from table to sink and back again, looking for handouts. Mitch calls him the hairy vacuum sweeper. Mitch. Oh, Mitch, hurry up!

By ten after eight, all the dishes were done, even the greasy frying pan left over from breakfast, but Mitch still wasn't home.

"I'm not going to wait any longer," I said. "I'm going to

call Billy and tell him that I have to talk to Mitch right now."

I had to dial twice: The first time Billy's line was busy; when I dialed again, Billy's mom answered the phone. Mrs. Hunt is really nice. You'd never guess she was Peabrain's mother. Once in the Kroger store, we had an interesting conversation about UFO's. She believes in them too, but she wasn't nice tonight. As soon as I asked to speak to Billy, her voice became cold and businesslike, just like Mom's when strange girls call to talk to Mitch. She didn't even let me explain who I was. "Mrs. Hunt? Wait." But she'd already hung up.

"What happened?" Ivy said. "How come you didn't talk to Billy?"

"He wasn't there," I said slowly. "Mrs. Hunt said he wasn't home."

"Not home?"

I shook my head. "She said he was over at a friend's house. For dinner."

Seventeen

The Last Resort

"But...but..." Ivy sounded like a motor boat running out of gas. If this weren't so serious, it would have been funny. "But you heard what your mom said. Mitch is supposed to be over there for dinner."

"I know, but Mrs. Hunt said he was over at a friend's."

"Well, that doesn't make sense. If they're not over here and they're not over there, then where are they?" Ivy sounded mad, as if it were all my fault that Mitch and Pea-brain had disappeared.

"I don't know where they are." I was getting mad now too. "But I bet they're someplace where they're not supposed to be!"

I marched over to the screen door and looked out. The light was fading from the sky. From down the street, I could hear Baby Imogene fussing. Bedtime. Even the robins were gone from the lawn. I looked at the clock again. It was almost eight-thirty. In another hour it would be dark.

A friend's house, Mrs. Hunt had said. Which friend? Mitch had lots of friends from school, but lately he and

Billy were always together. Mitch didn't even talk about any other friend except...except for Sam Toro. But who was he? We still didn't know a thing about him.

A moth fluttered against the screen. Ivy came and stood beside me. "Lizzie?" Her voice was hesitant. "You don't think they're at the Wentworth place, do you?"

"The Wentworth place? Tonight?" The idea had never occurred to me. "No, they wouldn't go there! Remember what Billy said?"

"I know, but that's just it. He said nobody should ever go there because it's so scary and all, but they were there today and they weren't scared and..." Ivy twisted the string necklace around her finger until her finger turned bright red. "...and I've been thinking that maybe they made the whole story up. Maybe they just said the place was haunted to keep us away from there."

"Made it up! No, they—" But now that she had said it, I knew that was exactly what I'd do if I wanted to keep people away. I'd make up some phony-baloney ghost story and—"Boy, if that's true!" It made me cringe to think Ivy might be right. Maybe that was why Mitch didn't want to talk about it. Maybe all that moaning and squeaking never really happened except in Peabrain's head. "Just wait until I see those guys! They're going to be sorry."

"Don't get mad, Lizzie. You know Mitch wouldn't tell a fib like that. I mean, not without a good reason."

I snorted. Ivy would defend Mitch even if he robbed the Broadhead bank. "The bank!" I said. Ivy stared at me. "Maybe that's why Mitch didn't want us around the Wentworth place. He didn't want us to see something—or someone."

"The mysterious stranger," Ivy breathed. Involuntarily I glanced overhead, thinking of the pillowcase hidden in Mitch's closet. I felt sick to my stomach. It all seemed to lead to the same conclusion: Mitch and the mysterious stranger.

"Lizzie, we can't wait any longer. We have to go look for them." Ivy's voice was urgent. "Mitch might be in trouble, real trouble. If he's really mixed up with that man, they could send him to prison."

"Prison!" Then I caught myself. "No, they don't send kids to prison—do they?"

"They might," Ivy said. "Or reform school. Oh, Lizzie, that would be awful. Poor Mitch. We have to warn them. We just have to. They probably think this man is their friend!"

"But we don't know that's where they are," I said weakly.

Ivy jutted out her chin. "Where else could they be?"

I didn't know. But the Wentworth place! I thought of the long walk through the fields and then that great big empty house. What if—There was a sudden thump behind us. I jumped and whirled around. It was just Basil under the table looking for more crumbs.

"Basil, you dummy!" I yelled. Basil ducked his head, his tail drooping. He looked like I'd just beaten him. "Oh, I'm sorry." I went over and gave him a hug. "You're not really a dummy." But my heart was still thudding against my ribs.

"Lizzie?"

"All right. I'll go."

She nodded as if she knew that's what I was going to say all along. "We can take Basil with us too," she said. "Just in case..."

She didn't finish and I didn't want her to. "Okay," I said quickly.

We started out the door, but then I remembered something. "Wait a second." I raced upstairs and brought down my flashlight. It felt solid and heavy in my hand. "All right, I'm ready."

Fireflies flew up in the grass in front of us like tiny sparks. Baby Imogene must have fallen asleep. The only sounds we heard as we started down the alley were the clink of Basil's license tags and the soft call of a mourning dove.

I stopped behind Mrs. Nelson's rosebushes and tested the flashlight just to make sure it still worked. We were going to be home before it got really dark, but still...

We crossed Williams Road and started up the path, our feet kicking up the powdered dry dirt.

"You don't have to hold on to Basil's collar like that," I told Ivy. "He won't run away."

"I know." But she didn't let go.

Behind us, I could hear the ting-ting of the ice cream truck.

"I wish we were home," I whispered.

"Me too."

The moon was up. It was a thin, pale sliver in the sky, but the breeze as it blew over the fields was still oven-hot. I licked my lips nervously. They felt dry and dusty. "I don't see them, do you?"

Ivy shook her head. "No, not yet."

The long line of poplars drew closer. We slowed down. It was getting darker by the second.

I caught myself looking over my shoulder. I couldn't stop thinking of the mysterious stranger. What if he were here in the fields? Or at the house? Then what would we do?

"Do you see . . . anybody?" I didn't want to say his name out loud.

Ivy silently shook her head.

When the path swerved, we had to leave it and wade through the weeds. Even though it made it harder, we walked three abreast, with Basil in the middle.

At the black iron fence we stopped. The house looked bigger at night—much bigger. Its steep peaked roof was black against the sky. The porch under its round tower was filled with shadows. My heart began to pound. Was the front door open just a crack? I squinted up my eyes but it was too dark to see for sure. No, it had to be closed, I told myself. Billy made the whole story up. But it had been easier to be sure of that in my own kitchen than out here in the fields. Then I thought of the other stories—the tiny flickering lights in the attic, the bloodstains in the cellar. Were they all just figments? I moved closer to Basil and clutched the flashlight a little tighter.

"I don't see anything, do you?" My voice had a funny quiver in it.

"No." Ivy's lips barely moved. I could tell she was scared too.

Keeping close to the protection of the trees, we crept around to the side of the house.

"Look!" Ivy grabbed my arm, but I had seen it too. A light. A faint light coming from the cellar windows. We dropped down on our knees. A ghost? Could it be the Wentworth ghost? Ivy and I didn't move. The light didn't move either. That gave me the courage to crawl closer, pushing the weeds aside with my hands. Ivy followed right behind me, one hand on Basil's neck. The cellar windows were streaked with grime. I crawled a little closer. Holding my breath, I peeked in.

Eighteen

Sam Toro!

It was Mitch! Mitch and Peabrain. They were standing with their backs to the window, bending over a cluttered table. Three Boy Scout lanterns hanging from overhead pipes lit up the center of the room.

I let out a sigh of relief. They were okay. Nothing awful had happened to them after all. Deep down inside I'd been afraid that Mitch had really disappeared and I'd never see him again.

Peabrain must have said something funny just then because Mitch threw back his head and let out that loud he-he laugh of his.

Boy, here we had been worrying our heads off and look at them. Laughing and having a great time. I'd show them. I raised my hand to rap on the window. Then I had a better idea. We should give *them* a taste of the Wentworth ghost. It would serve them right. All it would take was a little moaning and door slamming.

I turned to whisper to Ivy when Mitch suddenly flinched and looked up at the ceiling. His head moved toward the stairs. Footsteps? Did he hear footsteps? I held my breath, listening.

The door opened at the top of the cellar steps. A thin pencil of light shone down. Then a voice called out, "Okay, you kids. What do you think you're doing down there?"

A pair of black shoes and legs in green trousers started down the stairs. Thud. Thud. Thud. Slow, heavy steps I could hear through the glass. The beam of light bounced over Mitch's upturned face, then Billy's.

"Who are you?" Mitch's voice rose and cracked.

The man stepped under the glow of the lanterns. We saw his face. Then the gun.

"It's him!" Ivy and I scrambled backwards from the window. I felt as if someone had punched me in the stomach. Think, think, I told myself frantically, but my mind was blank.

Basil knew something was wrong. He whined softly and tried to lick my face. "Shhh!" I covered his muzzle with my hand. "Shhh!" What if the man had heard him? I sat up, rigid with fear. Ivy lifted her head, listening too. A mourning dove called. There wasn't a sound from the house.

"The police," I whispered. It was hard to breathe. "Take Basil and get the police."

"But Mitch—"

"I know; I won't leave them." I shoved the flashlight into her hands. "Hurry! Hurry before it's too late."

I crouched in the weeds watching until I couldn't pick out Ivy's white blouse in the gloom. Basil had loped off ahead of her. Now I was all alone. I shivered in spite of the warmth. How could I have been so dumb? I should have told Mom and Dad everything at dinner tonight. I should have told Billy's mom when I called. I should have told *somebody*. If anything happened to Ivy, nobody would know where to look for us. It would be hours, maybe days, before anyone thought of the Wentworth place.

Oh, hurry, Ivy. Please hurry! I followed her in my mind's eye. She wouldn't even be at Williams Road yet. It would be ten, fifteen minutes before she could get to a phone.

99

I looked toward the house. The light from the lanterns glowed softly in the darkness. Silence. What was happening down there? What was he doing to them? I couldn't stand not knowing. Slowly, on my hands and knees, I started crawling back toward the light.

The dry weeds brushed against my face and caught in my hair. I forced myself to peek through the window. Mitch? I inched closer. Then I saw him. He was on the floor, his hands tied behind his back. In the shadows was Billy, his eyes squeezed shut as the man knelt beside him tying his hands too.

Don't hurt them, I prayed. Don't—Something wet and cold touched my leg. I yelped and rolled over. Basil! It was just Basil, but it was too late.

"All right," the man yelled. "All right. Whoever's out there, come down here or these boys will be sorry."

I stood up. I wanted to run, but I knew I couldn't leave Mitch and Billy down in that cellar. Basil pushed his nose against my hand. "Go home, Basil." I shoved him away. I didn't want him to get caught too. "Go find Ivy. Go on."

My legs felt rubbery. I wasn't sure that they would hold me. Using both hands, I felt my way along the side of the house. The back door was open a crack. Inside, the house was pitch dark except for the faint light at the bottom of the cellar stairs.

"Down here," the voice commanded.

I clung to the banister as I slowly made my way down.

"Lizzie!" Mitch's face was paper-white.

"Soooo, it's the little girl who lost her cat," the man said. "Where's your friend? The little skinny one?"

"She's home," I said, hoping it was true. Maybe she had already called the police. Maybe the police were—

Suddenly I realized that he was moving toward me. In his hand was a long piece of rope.

"No." I backed away, edging around the clutter of old furniture and boxes. "No." I bumped into the table.

"Look out!" Mitch said.

I whirled around. On the table was a huge glass aquarium. Even as I ducked around it, putting it between the man and me, I thought, so that's where Mitch hid it! But the next moment I realized something was *in* the aquarium. I saw a large, triangular head. A flickering tongue touched the glass. The whole bottom of the aquarium moved in a slow, huge coil.

"SNAKE!" I screamed and shoved it away.

The man jumped back, but not fast enough. The aquarium fell like a boulder at his feet and smashed into a million, trillion pieces.

There was stunned silence. Then from the floor came the sound of heavy breathing. *Haaaarrrrrrrrrrr.*

"Look out!" I yelled. The ground under the table seemed to be moving. "IT'S LOOSE!"

"Run!" Mitch shouted at the man. "It's coming after you."

The man took two fast steps backwards and turned toward the stairs. There was a faint tinkle of broken glass from the floor. *Haaarrrrrrr!*

The man whirled around, his arm outstretched. I saw a flash of steel in his hand. Then he fired.

The sound of the gun going off made my head snap. From somewhere outside, as if in answer, came the high, shrill sound of a police whistle.

"Police!" I screamed. "It's the police!"

The man let out a muffled oath and dashed up the stairs, his footsteps shaking the house.

"Untie me, Lizzie!" Mitch twisted around on the floor. "Hurry!"

I took a step forward, my foot crunching on the glass, and stopped. No, the snake! I peeked under the table expecting to see it shot to bits, but it was gone. Gone! My toes curled up my shoes. Where'd it go? The floor was littered with boxes and piles of stuff. It could be anywhere.

"Lizzie, hurry!"

Praying the snake had crawled off to die, I ran over to the boys and struggled to untie Mitch. Again and again I heard the blast of the police whistle. It was coming closer and closer. "We're down here," I yelled.

When I freed Mitch's arms, we jerked Billy to his feet and pushed him ahead of us up the stairs.

There was the thud of running feet overhead, and then there was Ivy at the top of the stairs. Behind her was Mrs. Nelson in her ruffled pink housecoat and running shoes.

"Ivy!" I pushed past Billy and grabbed her into a bear hug. Then I hugged Mrs. Nelson. Everybody was hugging everybody, except Billy, who still had his hands tied.

Mitch twisted his head around. "Hey, where are the police?"

"Ah..." Ivy blushed. From the long string around her neck she held up a whistle. A shiny Boy Scout whistle. "That was me."

Mitch's smile faded. "You mean, the police aren't coming?"

"I called them," Mrs. Nelson said, her voice quavered. "I did call them."

Still bunched together, we stepped cautiously out on the porch. I knew we were all thinking the same thing: What if he comes back?

"Look," Ivy whispered. From over the top of the hedge we saw one silent police car after another pulling off the highway and onto the dirt road. The door of the first car swung open before it came to a stop.

"They did come!" Mrs. Nelson gave a shout. "You-whooo! He went that way." She waved her arm toward the border of trees.

"And he's got a gun!" I yelled after her.

Mrs. Nelson caught the collar of her housecoat. "I wish I had worn my good blue one. Do you think they brought a photographer?" She herded us toward the police cars.

"Wait." Mitch turned back toward the house. "We can't leave Toro. Something might happen to him."

"Toro? Sam Toro?" I said. "Was he tied up down there too?"

Mitch looked at me as if I was crazy. "Toro?" Then he

started to laugh. He whacked Billy on the back. "Is he tied up down there too?" he mimicked.

"What?" I demanded. "What's so funny?"

"Sam Toro is the snake, Lizzie. A *bull* snake!"

"You mean, that *thing* was Sam Toro?" I couldn't believe it. I had spent all this time trying to track down a snake.

Nineteen

The End of the Story —Almost

"I didn't scream because I was scared," I carefully explained. Mitch rolled his eyes at me, but I ignored him. "The snake just surprised me, that's all."

It was after midnight but everyone was still sitting around our kitchen table: Mom, Dad, Mitch, Billy Hunt and his mom, Ivy and Chris Featherstone, and Mrs. Nelson. Chief of Police Travis had just left.

"I'd think finding yourself face-to-face with a wild snake would be enough to make anyone scream," Dad said.

"No, you should have seen her," Billy said. "She was great. First she let out this holler that would have shriveled your ears and then CRASH! She practically dumped the aquarium right over on him. That did it! That guy couldn't get out of the cellar fast enough, especially after Toro did his heavy breathing trick. He thought Toro was going to eat him alive!"

I looked to see if Billy was teasing me about deliberately

pushing the aquarium over, but he looked completely serious. I could feel my face getting red. I hadn't really been all
that brave. "It's Ivy who should get most of the credit," I
said. "She's the one who ran for help and then blew the
whistle. He thought it was the police, and then he really did
run."

"But why didn't you kids tell us about this man?" Mom
said. "Didn't you realize how dangerous all this spying and
crime-solving was? Good grief, something terrible could
have happened! And you never should have gone near that
abandoned house in the first place. You both know better
than that."

I looked at Mitch. I had a feeling that after tonight we
were both going to be grounded forever.

"They did try to tell me," Chris said. He looked really
embarrassed. "But I thought they were playing some kind
of game."

"It's a good thing *I* took them seriously." Mrs. Nelson
sniffed. "If I hadn't been paying attention—"

There was a sudden knock on the back door. We all
jumped. It even scared Basil. He let out a high bark. Dad
and Chris Featherstone went to the door together.

"Good grief," Mom said.

It was Gretchen Thomas from the *Broadhead Tribune*.
She started talking as soon as Dad opened the door. "My
husband's cousin was playing bridge at Police Chief
Travis's house when the call came in from the police station, and she called me." She sounded out of breath, as if
she'd been running. "I've already been down at the station,
but I just couldn't wait until morning to get the whole story.
A bank robber in Broadhead! That's front-page news!" She
flicked open her notebook. "Now tell me exactly what happened."

When Police Chief Travis had asked that question in his
big bull-froggy voice, we had gone around the table politely
taking turns, but now the sound of all our voices at once
started Basil barking again.

105

"It all began the night Mr. Bennett came to dinner," I said.

"No, no," Mitch interrupted. "It began way before that. It started when Billy and I wanted to buy Toro—that's our bull snake—but our parents said no, but it was sort of too late because we'd already paid for him and . . ."

"And asked afterwards," Dad said a little grimly.

"But we were hoping they'd change their minds." Mitch didn't look at Dad. "So we decided to hide Toro in the cellar of the Wentworth place. It was the only place we could think of that was close by and where nobody would find him. Gee, we sure never expected any of this! In fact, everything seemed to be going just fine until Lizzie and Ivy started snooping—"

Snooping! I opened my mouth to yell but he had already corrected himself. "I mean, hanging around. Anyway, after that Billy made up this story to scare them off, but he really overdid it. Creaking doors and ghosts and the whole bit. That just made everything worse."

Billy wiggled in his chair with embarrassment.

I surprised myself by saying, "Oh, I don't know. It was a pretty good ghost story. *Some* people would have believed it."

"So all along, it seems you boys were sharing the Wentworth place with a bank robber. For heaven's sake!" Gretchen Thomas scribbled a few more words in her notebook. "'Boys, bull snake and bank robber share ravaged mansion.'" She looked pleased with herself.

Dad caught my eye and winked.

"Of course we didn't know he was there," Mitch said quickly. "Billy and I always used the outside cellar door." He looked at Mom. "It wasn't locked or anything. And we never went upstairs. Gosh, we didn't even know the Green Pillowcase Bandit existed until tonight. When Police Chief Travis told us who he was, I couldn't believe it."

"But what about the green pillowcase upstairs in the closet?" I demanded. "When we found it, Ivy and I were scared silly that—"

Mitch swung around. "Have you been sneaking around in my room again?"

"We weren't sneaking," I said. "Besides, we only did it for your own good."

"But we *found* that pillowcase," Billy said. "It was under one of the porch bushes at the Wentworth place. It made a great snake bag. We used it to carry Toro home from the store."

A snake bag! And to think I'd picked it up.

"Then it's probably *the* green pillowcase!" Mrs. Nelson shouted. "Let's see it."

When Mitch brought it down from his room, everyone wanted to touch it except for me—and Dad. "I'll pass," he said. "Fingerprints, you know."

"Can you really take fingerprints from cloth?" Billy asked, but Mrs. Nelson interrupted him. "So there I was tonight," she called across the table to Gretchen Thomas, "all alone with Missy Megs when I saw two quick flashes of light in the alley right behind my rosebushes. I didn't even stop to think. I said, 'Delight, you have to call the police this minute and tell them those vandals are back.' Of course, I didn't know then that those two boys"—she nodded toward Mitch and Billy,—"were the source of those lights the first time."

Mitch had already explained to Chief of Police Travis that he and Billy had slipped out a couple of times at night the week before to double-check on Toro and make sure he wasn't cold. When Mom heard that, she'd clutched at her hair. "What would have happened if you had run into that ...that thug!" she said. "You could have been kidnapped. Or shot!" I thought it was pretty dumb too, even if the mysterious stranger hadn't been lurking around. I couldn't imagine walking way out there in the dark just to see if a snake was cold or not. But that was just like Mitch. He has a one-track mind. That also explained where he was last Sunday when I spent half the night waiting up for him.

Mrs. Nelson was still talking a mile a minute. "So I quick dialed 911, but of course they said that bobbing lights

107

in some alley were *not* an emergency and that they'd send someone when they could. Well!" she slapped her hand down on the table. "I waited and waited, but it seemed like they were never coming; so I'd just stepped outside to see what I could find out for myself when I saw little Ivy Featherstone running for dear life down the alley. 'Call the police,' she yelled. 'Call the police. He's caught Mitch and Billy in the cellar!'"

"I didn't really yell," Ivy said. "I just said 'Call the police.'"

"So we ran inside," Mrs. Nelson went right on as if she hadn't heard her. "And I called the police again. This time I told them it was an emergency and they'd better get out here quick! I no sooner hung up the phone when Ivy bolted back out the door. What could I do? I couldn't let her go alone, so there we were out in the middle of the fields when we heard a gun shot. I almost fainted!" She patted the collar of her housecoat as if she still felt a little faint. "But then this child pulled out a police whistle from a string around her neck and blew it as if it were the Last Judgment."

"It's a Boy Scout whistle, not a police whistle," I said softly.

Ivy head me and blushed. She put her hand over the bump under her blouse.

"Good thinking, Ivy," Mitch said. "That really saved our necks."

Ivy beamed and ducked her head.

"But what I don't understand," Gretchen Thomas said, "is how did you girls suspect this pillowcase bandit in the first place?"

"Well..." Ivy and I took turns telling her all about our detective work. "Of course, we didn't know for sure he was the Pillowcase Bandit," I said modestly as I finished. "But we did know he was up to something suspicious."

"My!" Gretchen Thomas shook her head as if our story had taken her breath away. She started a new page in her notebook. "'Girls Save Bank, Brother and Friend From

Fiend.' Goodness, I wonder what Mr. Bennett will say when he finds out that you two girls have saved the bank!"

Dad reached over and squeezed my hand. "Given that it's Lizzie and Ivy, he won't even be surprised." Then he laughed. "Poor Wendell. He's had more than enough excitement for one night and now this."

"Excitement? What else happened tonight?" Now that it turned out that Ivy and I were right about the GPB, he couldn't get too mad about our notes.

"Not now," Mom said softly. "Later."

"Why not?" I asked when Gretchen pulled out a camera from her giant purse. "All right, let's have a big picture."

She arranged us by size. Ivy had to stand next to Mrs. Nelson. I had to stand on the other side.

"Say cheese," Gretchen called.

"CHEESE!"

The next afternoon, there we all were. Right on the front page of the *Broadhead Tribune*. Gretchen Thomas had even used one of my headlines: "Kids Catch Bandit!"

"Look, we're famous!" I told Ivy. And we were—well, pretty famous, anyway. I loved it. I spent the next couple of days, when I wasn't giving interviews, pasting all the newspaper articles into my scrapbook. We made both the *Detroit Free Press* and the *Detroit News* and even the *Chicago Tribune*. The *Green Hills Daily* called us "Junior Crime Stoppers." I really liked that one.

The Sunday edition of the *Broadhead Tribune* carried another big picture of us. This time Wendell Bennett was in it too. "Kids Awarded $500 From Grateful Bank President," it said in big, black letters. In the picture Mr. Bennett is shaking my hand, and Ivy is holding up her check for the camera and smiling. What the article didn't say was that the money had to go into a special education fund for college. I didn't mind too much. Mom and Dad have promised me a loan, so now I can finally buy my binoculars.

The last picture was of *him*. Link Smith, also known as

the mysterious stranger, also known as the Green Pillow-case Bandit. The police had caught him that very same night while Gretchen was still interviewing us. Upstairs in one of the bedrooms of the Wentworth place, the police had found a suitcase and cans of food. Ivy had been right about the house being his hideout. And Mom had been right about how dangerous it had been for Mitch and Billy. They could have run into him any one of those nights they had sneaked out to check on the snake. The thought still gave me the shivers.

"Want to see the scrapbook?" I asked Mitch. "I just finished putting everything in."

"Poor Toro." Mitch turned to the picture Gretchen Thomas had taken of all of us in the kitchen. Putting his finger in the space between his head and Billy's, he said, "He should be right there. He was part of all of this too."

I just nodded because I didn't want to hurt Mitch's feelings. I knew he felt really sad about losing his pet. He and Billy had gone back to Wentworth place the very next morning to look for him with Billy's mom and Chief of Police Travis, but the snake was gone. They'd been back every day since, too, but no Sam Toro. He had vanished without a trace.

"He could be anywhere," Mitch said glumly. "Any crack, any hole. We could spend the rest of our lives in that cellar and never find him."

"He's pretty big to lose," I said. "I bet he'll turn up." For Mitch's sake I sort of hoped that it was true.

Later that afternoon Mrs. Nelson came over to borrow Mom's typewriter. She announced that she was going to write a book about the notorious Green Pillowcase Bandit of Broadhead, Michigan.

"I have a feeling we're not even going to be in it," I told Mitch.

Mitch grinned. "Well, look at it this way, Lizzybeth, you don't want to become too famous. It would blow your cover as a crime investigator."

"Really?" Then I saw he was just teasing. "You should

talk!" I whacked him on the arm. "If it hadn't been for Ivy and me, you and Billy would probably still be tied up in that cellar!"

"You're right," Mitch said, suddenly serious. "I was never so scared in my whole life. You and Ivy...boy...you two were really something."

"Honest?"

"Honest."

I wished Ivy were here. This was better than any old check and all the newspaper articles in the world put together. "Well, I was pretty scared too," I admitted generously.

Mitch rolled his eyes. "I know," he said and began to squeal, "Snake! Snake!"

"I didn't sound like that, Mitchell Bruce! I didn't!"

But Mitch just laughed louder.

"Well, smarty, speaking of investigating, just what were you and Billy doing with Mrs. Nelson's cat up on the Indian Trail?"

That really caught him off guard. He stopped laughing and straightened up. "Ssssssh! Keep your voice down."

But I wouldn't let up. "Come on, Ivy and I saw you guys with her. You can't fool us."

"Well..." He looked a little embarrassed. "Toro is a constrictor, right? And he has to eat, right?"

"Right." Then I caught on. "Not Missy Megs! It wasn't going to eat *her,* was it?"

"Sssssssh! Of course not, dummy. We wouldn't do that. It's just that Toro liked his food live and Billy and I had used up all our money for the aquarium. Bull snakes are supposed to like eggs too, but he wouldn't eat the one we brought him so—"

I interrupted him. "Is that why you wanted to borrow money from me? To feed a snake?" What a waste of my eight dollars that would have been.

Mitch nodded impatiently. "But then we decided to borrow Megs. We thought that she could catch a field mouse, and then we'd give it to Toro."

111

I remembered that awful picture of that poor little mouse in Mitch's snake book. "Oh, that's really mean!"

"No, it's not. Bull snakes just like to eat mice, that's all. You eat cows."

"No, I don't. Well, not real live cows, anyway. I mean, they're not alive when *I* eat them." But then I had to ask. "Did she catch any? Mice, I mean?"

"Nope, not a thing."

"Good." Somehow that made me like Megs a little better.

Using a cat as a mousetrap to feed a snake. I shook my head. Amazing. But later that week I heard something even more amazing. And from Ivy.

Twenty

Worms and Wedding Bells

"Lizzie, wait up!"

I turned around, still holding on to Baby Imogene's hand. Ivy was running down the alley toward us, her hair flopping on her shoulders.

"Boy, am I glad to see you," I called.

"Worrrrrrm," Imogene whined. "No, worrrmm." She pulled on my hand and pointed to the clumps of field daisies across the road on the Indian Trail.

"No, those are flowers, Imogene," I said. "Daisies. Just a second and we'll go pick some for your mother. Wouldn't that be fun?"

Ivy caught up with us, and we crossed Williams Road together. "Your mom told me where you were," she said. She bent down. "Hello, Imogene."

"Noooo." Imogene shook her head. She was so hot, her curls stuck to her pink scalp in little spiral horns. "Noooo." She pulled loose from my hand and ran down the bike path ahead of us.

"Wait up, Imogene," I called. We started after her, but

that only made her run faster, so we slowed down again to a walk. Sure enough, she slowed down too.

"Mrs. Morely doesn't feel very well," I explained, "so I sort of volunteered to take care of Imogene for a couple of hours."

"Is she really sick?"

"Yes, I mean no." I was bursting to tell. "She has m-o-r-n—" I started to spell it out and then realized Imogene couldn't hear me anyway. "She has morning sickness!"

"Really?" Ivy looked to see if I was teasing. "She's going to have a baby?"

When I nodded, she said softly, "Gosh, can you imagine having *two* Baby Imogenes?"

We could see her ahead of us now on the path. She had found a stick from somewhere and was busy whacking the heads off the daisies.

"No, I can't," I said. "Absolutely not." That made us both laugh.

"Now wait until you've heard *my* news," Ivy said. She hugged herself. "Chris told me this morning. It's even going to be in tonight's newspaper!"

"What?" I asked. "What?"

Ivy danced around. "You'll never guess. Never, ever."

"Never guess what? *What?*"

That got Baby Imogene excited. She dropped her stick and started running farther down the path.

"Imogene, wait," I yelled.

"Mr. Bennett and Ev—" Ivy was laughing so hard that I missed the next of couple of words. She had to start over. "Mr. Bennett and EvaLynne are going to get married!"

"Worrrrrrm!" shouted Imogene.

"What?" I yelled. "Really? They're really going to get married?" EvaLynne Hayes and Mr. Bennett? I couldn't believe it. Then I thought of something that had been bothering me all along. "So that's why we saw him over at EvaLynne's house that Saturday. They must have been having a date!"

114

"And we thought they were talking about us!" Ivy started to laugh again.

"But what about your dad?" I asked. "Is he . . . ah . . . sad or anything?"

Ivy looked thoughtful. "No, he said she was a very nice person and that he hoped she'd be happy. But he's known for almost a week! Remember that night when EvaLynne called, and she just talked forever? Well, that's when she told him. She hadn't called about us at all."

"Worrrrrm!" shrieked Imogene. She waved a fistful of crushed daisies at us. She had gone farther than I had thought.

Ivy and I looked at each other and groaned. "I hope that by next summer she'll have a new word," I muttered.

"Just a minute, Imogene. We're coming," Ivy called, and we started to run.

"Worrrrrrm!" Imogene's voice was as shrill as a tea kettle whistle.

"You don't have to yell, we're right—Ohmygosh!" Ivy suddenly stopped. I ran into the back of her.

There sunning himself on the path, all four feet of him, was Mr. Sam Toro.

"I never thought I'd see him again," Mitch kept saying at the dinner table that night. "I never thought he'd ever turn up. Ever."

"Neither did I," Dad said.

"Maybe he missed you," Ivy offered. "Maybe he was looking for you and Billy."

I groaned, but Mitch looked pleased. He had spent all afternoon at Billy's house. Billy's mom had relented and said they could build a cage for Toro in their garage.

"Better theirs than mine," Dad had said when Mitch told him about it, so it looked like Toro was going to be around for a while.

"But how do you think he got out of the cellar?" I asked.

"Oh, snakes are really smart," Mitch bragged. "They can

squeeze through the tiniest places. I read about one that crawled up through a hole in the box springs of a mattress and hid out there for days until he got hungry. That's probably what happened to Toro. He probably got hungry and crawled out looking for some mice to eat. They like rabbits too. And rats. Billy says maybe we can raise white mice and feed—"

Dad cleared his throat and gently pushed his plate of untouched food away. Mitch didn't notice, but Mom did.

"Well, leave it to Imogene to be the one who found it," she said quickly. Then she giggled. "That child!"

Mom was in a great mood because she'd just found out that she'd gotten an A on her Jane Austen paper. It was the only A in the class. She said maybe she'd found her calling. Maybe she should write English papers for a living.

"And speaking of photographs," Dad said (which we weren't), "the announcement of EvaLynne's engagement is in tonight's newspaper." He passed it around the table. It was one of those couple pictures. Mr. Bennett had on a shiny blue suit and EvaLynne was smiling hard, you could almost see her curls bounce. "Happy Couple," read the caption beneath the picture.

"Well," Mom said. "Look on the bright side. Maybe now he'll give up those dreadful cigars."

Dad sighed. "They say love is blind."

I peeked over at Ivy. The bump under her blouse was still there. Love is blind, I thought, but at least this summer it didn't smell like Ivory soap.

"Lizzie, what are you thinking about so hard?" Dad asked.

I couldn't say love, so I said the first thing that popped into my head. "I was just wondering what's going to happen next summer, that's all."

"*Next* summer?" Mom said. "Wait, it's not even July yet. Besides, I'd think you've all had enough excitement to last a lifetime of summers."

"Oh, no," Mitch said just to tease her. "There can never

be too much excitement. Just think, maybe next summer Billy and I'll get another snake. Maybe a mate for Toro!"

"No, thanks," I said. "That isn't what *I* had in mind. No, leave it to Ivy and me. We'll think of something." I looked across the table at Ivy and grinned. "And I have a hunch it's going to be something...terrific!"